TO Joo.

MW00945568

THE ADVENTURES OF UNIQUE DOLLAR BILLY UDB BY SEA KAY

Laugh out Loud!

Hope you have as much fun
reading this book as
I had writing it.

Happy Reading!
Sea Kay

Sea Kay

THE ADVENTURES OF UNIQUE DOLLAR BILLY UDB

BY
SEA KAY

XULON PRESS

Xulon Press
2301 Lucien Way #415
Maitland, FL 32751
407.339.4217
www.xulonpress.com

Printed in the United States of America.

ISBN-13: 9781545648049

In memory of my mother who taught me to write.

This book is dedicated to my grandfather, from whom I have probably inherited my creative writing instincts, and to all fourth graders, especially the students at the Cherokee Elementary School, who have inspired me with their curiosity and ambition.

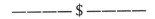 $

Introduction

———— ❋ ————

In my scientific career, I have published papers; however, I have never taken a creative writing class or written fiction, much less stories for children. One fine day, I decided I wanted to reach out to children by writing humorous stories to make them laugh and teach them some of life's important lessons.

This collection of children's short stories revolves around a one-dollar bill named Unique Dollar Billy (UDB) who lives with several families (in wallets, purses, and pockets) as he experiences what life has to offer. You will find him witnessing different aspects of life that we humans would find commonplace and ordinary. As UDB describes the circumstances around him, readers will see how unique and original these parts of life are and why we should pay attention to them for the future.

UDB spends time with four different families in this book. It is interesting to see the various ways they spend their time together and how they interact with each other. You will find UDB in school, on trips, in a traffic jam, understanding April Fool's Day, celebrating Halloween, in the farm with Grandparents and even getting accidently tossed in the garbage. While enjoying these experiences, UDB also learns valuable life lessons that he can impart to readers.

The character of UDB will engage children's imaginations and minds as they read his stories. It will bring his experiences to life for readers as they wonder where and how a dollar bill travels in this world.

My dream is to reach out to as many children as possible so we realize how each of us is as unique as UDB. Children, I hope you will have as much fun travelling with UDB as I did. Laugh out loud and enjoy my first book in the UDB series, *The Adventures of Unique Dollar Billy*. Happy reading!

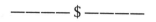

Acknowledgments

———✳———

I must thank my husband, Krish, for encouraging me to jot down my thoughts and not worry about editing or refining until later. It has given me immense joy to create Unique Dollar Billy (UDB) and write for children. I want children to laugh while reading about his travels and adventures. To reach out, I decided to have the manuscript edited by the younger generation and have the stories illustrated by them, too. I actually wanted to visualize the stories through their eyes.

Somehow I succeeded in recruiting Viha and Nammu to help with the editing. They have been very generous with their praise and suggestions. Talented illustrators, Anika and Anushka, were mentored by the older, accomplished girls, Juhi and Saveena. Taameen stepped in very proficiently for the finishing touches.

These young editors' and illustrators' imaginations have truly been my inspiration. I hope they had as much fun illustrating and editing as I had writing the stories. Thank you very much, girls, for your constant support. I am indeed indebted to each of you.

Many thanks are also due to Leslie Bassett and Katherine Larson, who read the edited manuscript and gave invaluable comments. My young students have offered me tremendous incentives to continue writing. I am constantly asked where UDB is off to next. The staff at Xulon Press have helped me very patiently through the whole process.

Thanks to all of you for the opportunity to discover the world through UDB.

Contents

———✳———

The Cherry Family

The Brown Family

The Deere Family

Universal

Dollar Billy Discovers He Is Unique Like You and Me

What is unique about a one-dollar bill? Every bill has a green background with the number 1 printed and spelled on one side, and George Washington's (the first president of the United States of America) face on the opposite side. Each bill has a distinctive number with some tiny signatures that cannot be read but that alone does not make it special. However, if you look closely, you will notice that every bill is indeed different. The travels and journeys of each bill have left distinctive marks on each of us. It is these different experiences that make us bills unique entities.

Here begins my story—or, shall I say, my adventures—as "Dollar Billy." I stay hidden in the wallet of my owner, My Lady, as I accompany her to church on Ash Wednesday. While dropping bills, she accidentally touches her forehead with the black ash mark before touching me. My friend, another dollar bill, is taken away and dropped into a collection basket for monetary donations while I am stained and feel forlorn.

On her way home, My Lady is thirsty and decides to taste the lemonade from a little girl's stand on the sidewalk. Guess what? I almost jump out of the wallet as I am used to pay for the lemonade. Immediately, the girl who receives me laughs out loud because I am stained black. Even my George Washington has a black eye. However, her friend tells her that if we can have a black president like Barack Obama, why not a blackened dollar bill? I am put into a box with the other bills, but I am scared to make friends in case they laugh at me too.

Once we get home, their mom gives the girls coins in exchange for my dollar bill, so the coins can be saved in a piggy bank. There are a lot of clinking and clanking noises as the change is swapped. Gosh, I did not realize how heavy and noisy coins can be! No wonder they call it chunk change.

I find myself squashed in between a $20 and a $10 bill in the mom's wallet. Feeling dejected, I scrunch up. Seeing my problem, the $10 bill stretches out and makes room for me. Taking the hint, the $20 bill stretches out even more and makes more room. They ask me why I am feeling so sad. When I tell them about my black eye, they laugh. The $20 bill shows me her blackened White House. It almost looks like a Black House! The $10 bill shows me his blackened face of Alexander Hamilton, the first US Secretary of the Treasury (the place where I was born). They make me realize that in comparison, new, crisp bills are rather bland and boring. From this, I understand that the more soiled and stained the bill, the wiser we become. Specific marks make each of our journeys through life indeed unique ones. No two bills have the same story to share. Now, this is an *aha* moment! I feel better already.

The $20 and $10 bills not only stretch, but totally encircle me. I no longer feel alone or isolated. I truly feel like part of a family. The words "In God We Trust" fold around me. It all makes sense now! My uniqueness is what it is all about. I am indeed proud to say that from here on, I plan to be "Unique Dollar Billy"!

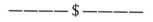

Activities

1. What makes you unique? Identify one thing about yourself that makes you unique.

2. Ask your parents what is unique about you and share your ideas with them.

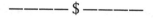

UD Billy Meets New Friends

I am lovingly called UD Billy (Unique Dollar Billy). Since each person has a name, why not me? I'm still getting used to it, though. I think I am an introvert, as I tend to withdraw and scrunch up. Introvert or extrovert—it does not matter. I am happy with who I am, and that's what matters.

My Lady cashes a check at the local bank, and suddenly, I find that I must make room for more bills. She is in such a rush that she just stuffs them in her wallet any old way. This is the first time that I understand the meaning of the word "stifle." I am sure it means "crowded." There is no order to the bills. All of us are trying to stay calm and just fit in. This is hard work. I cannot scrunch up anymore, but I cannot complain; I am one of those near the edge, and can at least peek out. Seeing me wriggling and crackling, the bill next to me giggles. Now, you could ask, how do I know that she is a girl? Her George Washington has a strand of hair stuck to his ponytail. However, in those days, and even these days, men also wear ponytails. Not being sure, I gather the courage to ask her name.

She inches closer to me by stretching a little and tells me that her name is Billie May and that she is a girl. When I tell her my name, she says, "Oh how cute!" Her comment amazes me as I do not think being called UD Billy is all that cute. She wonders what the UD stands for. She asks if it is maybe Under Developed, or Upsy Daisy, or maybe even Up and Down?

When I tell her what the U stands for, she giggles again and says that it is *profound* to be "Unique." I wonder what *profound* means. I hope it means that I am a nice boy. I will have to look it up, as I do not have the nerve to ask her and feel foolish. From my sheepish grin, she gathers I am not a literature major, so she informs me that *profound* means great. Wow! I think being great is just great. I immediately make her my best *pro-found* friend. Remember now, I have made her only my best pro-found friend and not a con-found friend. Get it? It's about pros and cons!

She asks me if I am lonely. At times, I am, but before I can scrunch up any further, she introduces me to a dollar bill on her other side. This one flaps his free edge and introduces himself as August Bill. I find that he is unique, too; he has glasses drawn around his George Washington eyes! As if George needs glasses! For him to read what? These two seem to be really smart bills. I hope I can be friends with them.

Billie May explains that they are named according to their birth months, May and August. When is my birthday? Oh dear, I don't know. Billie May stretches and examines some numbers on all of us and declares that I have a number in the same series as August, just a 3 instead of August's 2 at the end. Wow! That means I was born (or printed) in August, too! Guess what? It is currently August, so we get to celebrate two birthdays this month!

Billie May gets excited, and with more giggles, she asks the $5, $10, and $20 bills to chip in for a party. With all her cleaning and stretching, she almost loses her necklace. All the bills in the wallet sing "Happy Birthday," and we all stretch out. Both August and I look straight and almost starched now.

August only looks nerdy with his spectacles. He is actually a great guy, or should I say a *profound* entertainer as his stories are hilarious. Billie May is easily excitable, and her funny giggle always puts us in a good mood so we're ready to have fun. I turn out to be the quiet troublemaker! In fact, I have recently learned to wink with my one good eye! Billie May makes me use this new talent of mine on her friends.

The three of us have become best buddies. We name ourselves "The Three Billeteers" like "The Three

Musketeers." That does sound funny and catchy. One with a black eye, one with a pony tail and one with spectacles on our respective George Washingtons. We do make quite a threesome. Making new friends is always fun and so exciting. They say, "birds of a feather flock together." We dollar bills are clones, but still, each of us is one of a kind. Is that a *profound* statement or what?

Questions

1. What name would you choose for your group of best buddies?

2. What do you think *friendship* means?

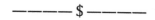

3

UDB Rides the Local Bus

I have seen sights, some beautiful and some not so great. I have heard sounds you might never have heard, and some you may never hear. I listen to secrets—mostly pleasant scenes, but some have been ugly and scary. You might think I am lucky for having so many different experiences.

Let me tell you about my ride on the public bus. The $20 and $10 bills surrounding me are not excited at all. They tell me to be prepared to move on and bid me goodbye. They hug me and go right back to sleep. However, I am too hyper to sit scrunched up in my owner's wallet. Being eager to see the world, I peek out. Lo and behold, I hear a bus stop. My owner climbs onto the bus, pulls me out, and drops me into a box near the driver. I assume that he is the driver, as I hear him shut the door. I fall into a dark pit, or what feels like a pit of coins. My, my, how noisy the coins are! The little copper one-cent ones make the most noise. It is difficult to imagine that coins are almost a tenth or twentieth my size and can still make so much noise. With coin-friends meeting after a long time and talking over one another, you can imagine the sound: *clink, clank, clink, clank.* I am quite sure no one is listening. It sounds like a lot of greetings are being exchanged. Oh well. I guess I am not too good at their coin language. Wait, who do I see? Two of my old friends, with whom I have shared wallet space before.

We have even shared some rides in the past. Before we can exchange stories, the bus takes off.

Now, close your eyes and imagine you are on a bus. What sounds do you hear? Then, close your ears and look around. What do you see? Observe the traffic and the drivers of other vehicles on the road. I bet you see buildings of all sizes, playgrounds, malls, shopping centers, and people buzzing around. What are the names of the trees and flowers you are passing?

Now, look around at the passengers in the bus and imagine their journeys through life. Some are napping with their mouths open and heads tilted back. It is actually funny to see their heads roll with the movement of the bus. Oh my. I hear a man snoring! Beside him, a little boy with his face turning red—probably his grandson—is trying to wake him up rather unsuccessfully! Some people are just blankly staring out the window. I bet they don't know where they are. They are probably lost in their thoughts and not even aware of the passing scenes. Others are looking at their watches, hoping to make it to their appointments on time. They are afraid that being late to work may cost them their jobs. Some ladies at the back are gossiping quite loudly and shaking their hands around, while the younger crowd—the mobile telephone users—are busy texting away.

Oh dear. A bunch of unruly, loud teenagers are boarding. I hope they behave and talk quietly, or else the driver will stop the bus. The teens make their way to the middle of the bus and start shouting at one another. They let their backpacks fall with huge thuds as they get ready for a fist fight on the bus. The driver senses trouble and pulls over. He enters the aisle and tells the teens to calm down. Just then, a brave young Girl Scout, accompanying a blind elderly lady with a cane marked with red towards the bottom, stands up and, in a calm tone, tells the teens to take their seats. She tells them that the passengers on the bus are both young and old, and we must respect the rights of all the people on board. She then points to the lady with the cane with the red markings and tells them to respect people with disabilities like partial blindness, too. Fighting will only stop or delay the ride, and people will not be able to get to their appointments on time.

Hearing her calm voice, the teenagers sheepishly pick up their backpacks and take their seats at the back of the bus. It took a little girl to bring them to their  senses. I would like to hug the Girl Scout. In my opinion, she deserves a Medal of Honor. What guts to stand up to teenagers bigger and older than her and request that they behave properly! Now that is enough excitement for one day.

While we are being lulled to sleep on the ride, the bus comes to a halt. All passengers are told to get off. I see the Girl Scout escort the old lady off the bus. The teenagers get off the bus quietly after them. I think that I saw them smiling at one other. They were probably good friends just having a small misunderstanding leading to a big fight.

The driver collects the fares in the box, moves us to a bag, and hands it over to another person. Finally, we are separated from those noisy coins. Phew, what a relief! We are taken to the bank, where we are separated into cozy $1 bundles. I have met so many friends today. I am so happy. My exciting experiences with humans show on me, through my different marks. But that is what makes my journey different. That is what makes me unique!

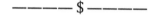

Activities

1. Do you want to be a Girl/Boy Scout? If so, discuss your ideas with your parents.

2. When boarding a vehicle, be it a car, bus or train, be kind and let the elders and disabled board ahead of you.

3. Keep a log of when you have been brave and stood up against what you think is wrong.

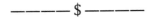

4

UDB Goes to a Conference

My Gentleman (MG) is a lovable, absent-minded scientist. He has been invited to give a talk at a conference. Until the last minute, he is preparing his presentation and asks his wife (ML) to help him pack his clothes. He finds that he has not withdrawn money to pay for the taxi and other travel expenses. ML sees his plight and, smiling, lends him money from her wallet. I am one of the bills she parts with. Although I will really miss her and the family, I realize I need to grow up and be a big boy. No tears but a last peek at them to say goodbye. Who knows where life will lead us? I may land up in one of their pockets again. The little children will have grown up and I may be a wrinkled old man by then. But first things first, I need to enjoy my youth!

I start to get excited in MG's wallet as I still have some of my friends and elders ($20 Mother March (MoMa) and $10 bills) with me. He is running a bit late, so he rushes out the door, kissing ML and the children. He instructs the taxi driver to take him to Dulles Airport in metropolitan Washington, DC. Just as the taxi pulls out the driveway, he sees ML running to the car waving her arms to stop. He has forgotten his bags! The driver helps him load them in the trunk and we are off to the airport. I am not one of the bills used to pay for the taxi, so I find myself in the United Airways line. When it is MG's turn, the check-in lady informs him that his flight is from Reagan National Airport and not Dulles!

MoMa asks if I knew that metropolitan Washington DC is serviced by three airports; Baltimore Washington International (BWI), Reagan National, and Washington Dulles International. I tell her that I have visited all three airports. All are about a forty-minute drive from one another in different directions. Oh dear! MG has arrived at the wrong airport! The check-in lady at Dulles helpfully points him to a shuttle that can take him to Reagan National. When MG arrives at National, he rushes to catch his plane but finds that he is too late. It has already taken off! The check-in gentleman at National instructs him that the last flight to his destination today is from BWI. Oh my! BWI is the furthest away among the three airports. Fortunately, there are almost four hours to catch the flight. This time, he is instructed to take the BWI shuttle.

Wait a minute! Just then, MG realizes that in his haste, he has left his bags on the shuttle bus that took us to Reagan National. He now must wait a half hour until the shuttle returns to recover his baggage.

This is hilarious! We could have taken off from all three DC airports within a span of a few hours in one day! Finally, MG manages to check his baggage at BWI, and we are on time for this flight. He is told that he is lucky as this is a direct International flight. He would have to make connections from the other airports. At the waiting area, MG is so deeply immersed in his work that he does not hear the boarding announcement. We are anxious in his wallet, but don't  know how to help. I plan to accidently tip the wallet over so it falls out of his pocket. Knowing MG, even that would not help. He is so seriously absorbed in his work. Oh dear. Are we ever going to get there? I am very anxious now.

Finally, MG looks up and hears his name announced, saying it is the last call. He jumps up and runs to board the flight. This time, he takes his carry-on baggage with him, looking back to make sure he has left nothing behind. Before boarding, he is asked for his passport. Rather surprised by this routine request, he desperately searches his carry-on bag. It is a big mess now. His ironed clothes are ruffled and his toiletries are almost falling out of the bag. The passport is not there. He somehow manages to shut the bag. He then looks for his passport in his wallet, although it is not among us. He is worried now and sweating. An officer calmly asks him to step aside and look in his computer bag. Sure enough, it is there. Quickly, he hands it over to the security officer. However, he is informed that it is not his passport! What? Now, wait a minute—this is scary and unreal. Will they lock him up or put him in jail?

Surprisingly, the passport he is holding is his wife's. How could this happen? MG is really puzzled, as he had produced his passport while checking in his bags. He searches once more in his computer bag and finds another passport. This time he checks to make sure it is definitely his. He remembers that when ML saw a passport near his forgotten bags at home, she handed it to him, assuming he had forgotten it with his bags. The officer smiles on seeing the frazzled professor, who remarks that today he has had many episodes but this one absolutely takes the cake! MG is then subjected to another security check before they allow him to board. We bills are crossing over each other hoping he will not be stopped this time.

Finally, after what seems like ages, we are seated and belted. The plane backs up a short distance. Did you know that planes do not have a reverse gear? I guess they don't need them except to get out of their landing spots. A little motorized vehicle helps with that. We are now on our way. At least, I think so.

Gosh, I did jinx it. We are stuck on the tarmac. A huge line of planes after and before us. Now what? The pilot announces that there is an imminent severe thunderstorm and the tower is not permitting any planes to land or take off. Looking on the positive side, it must be fun to be in charge at the tower. It must feel like playing musical chairs with the planes landing and taking off.

The storm hits with force, but we are all seated in the plane, on the ground, so there is no turbulence. I can hear hail on the roof of the plane. However, it passes in fifteen minutes, and we are cleared for take-off. At our destination, after claiming baggage, MG takes a taxi to the hotel. As luck would have it, I will be attending the conference with MG after all; he uses his plastic card to pay for the taxi ride.

Hotels no longer give their guests actual keys; the doors open with card keys. MG has trouble with his card until he figures out the system. We are now in a nice room, but there is no light. The card key needs to be inserted in a slot adjacent to the door for power in the room. MG puts the key there and goes back out to get his baggage. Meanwhile, the door shuts behind him with his key inside. Oh dear. He must stand in line again at the desk with his baggage and get another key made! I think that MG really needs a good night's sleep so he can function tomorrow.

This has been an exciting day so far. What a ride with MG! What an absent-minded fellow he is. We all miss ML so much. I am sure he will give a brilliant talk and be surrounded by students tomorrow. That should bring him back down to earth. However, I will say that traveling with absent-minded professors is a lot of fun—always unpredictable and hilarious!

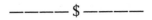

Activities

1. Before a trip, make a list of things you will need to take with you. Be sure to review the list with your parents. Post it on the refrigerator door.

2. What has been your favorite trip so far, and why? Draw a picture of your favorite trip.

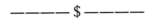

5

UDB Runs to the Ice Cream Truck

Who doesn't like ice cream? If you ask me, I can have ice cream any time of the day. After all, eating ice cream is what summer is all about. Have you noticed that flavors vary according to personalities? Let me give you a few examples, although you may not agree with me. Do you think cookies and cream is a favorite with disciplined people who think black is black and white is white, and there is no grey? Do envious people choose pistachio because it is green in color? Do girls choose pink sprinkles? Do boys who love playing baseball choose Baseball Nut? Do sour-faced people choose key lime pie because it tastes quite tart? Do sweet talking people like sticky caramel crunch? Maybe good-natured and bland people favor plain vanilla. At this rate, I bet we could come up with a lot of such combinations!

Upon hearing the ice cream truck song, "Pop Goes the Weasel," I almost jump out of my owner's wallet. I am so in the mood for ice cream. It is a hot day and the extreme humidity is making me feel lazy. My owner, Mom Pond, hands me and my friend, another $1 bill (AB, August Bill) to her daughter, little Mary, to get some ice cream. Mary runs up to the truck but is

27

unable to decide what flavor she wants. I wish she would hurry up and decide.

The new ice cream truck is painted red, white and blue with ice cream flavors written all over it in attractive, fanciful colors. These new trucks not only serve the old ice cream bars but have buckets of ice cream flavors to choose from. I assume the huge modern freezers help create these new additions. There are too many choices these days! It's very confusing!

Mary meekly asks if she could try some flavors? With gusto, the ice-cream man offers her two mini scoops of the Triple Berry Munchie and Heavenly Mango Orange flavors. My friend and I get to taste both, as Mary's grubby fingers and the hot sun melt the tasting portions immediately. I'm not complaining any more about becoming sticky. I am not too fond of berries, but the Mango Orange turns out to be as heavenly as promised. I hope Mary chooses it.

I am kept in great suspense, but I learn a big lesson that day. As Mary steps back to decide, she notices a sad little boy sitting on the curb with a cute dog beside him. Mary walks up to him and asks him why he is sad. Apparently, his mother rushed out to work in the morning, forgetting to leave him his promised ice cream money. Mary has two of us dollar bills with her and offers to share us with him. He refuses the offer, as his parents have told him not to accept anything from strangers. Mary immediately introduces herself to the boy, John. They find they are the same age and live just two doors away from each other, on the same street. Now they are no longer strangers. Mary also tells him that her Mom had given her a dollar for ice cream and another dollar for helping to fold the laundry yesterday. So, she is technically offering John the money she earned doing chores. John jumps up excitedly, ready to order ice cream.

I am left in suspense once again! Fortunately, Mary chooses the Heavenly Mango Orange flavor that I was craving in a cone. By the time she hands me over to the ice cream man, I already have my fill of it. It is deliciously yummy. John turns out to love berries, so he goes straight for the Triple Berry Munchie. Strangely, he orders one scoop and politely requests that the ice cream man split it into two cups. Mary is surprised when John offers his first cup to his cute dog. He explains that they are so attached to each other that they always share their belongings.

Mary and John sit on a bench together, jabbering away, laughing, eating, and talking all at the same time. What a wonderful way to pass the time with new friends.

Meanwhile, I meet many of my old friends in the money box. The box is opened and closed so many times that day. The ice cream man is so happy to serve the huge line of children today. He is laughing and talking to all of them while piling us in his box.

The children are happy to meet their friends in the line while choosing their favorite flavors of ice cream. I am delighted to meet up with my old pals.

At the same time, Mary's baby sister, Cecily, is not happy to find her Mary outside eating ice cream. Mom Pond is forced to pick up the howling child and bring her to the truck for her share of ice cream. However, Mom does not have change for Cecily's ice cream. She hands the ice cream man $5, and guess what? We are handed back to her as change. Is this a coincidence or a miracle?

We are delighted to be right back where we started! The best part of my day was, of course, tasting the flavors. I am quite sticky by now, but happy and no longer listless. Enjoy the rest of the day, children. Remember to do some chores at home and earn more money for ice cream.

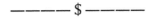

Activities

1. What is your favorite ice cream flavor?

2. Do you have a pet? If so, what is its name? Are you able to share any foods with your pet?

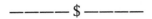

- 6 -

UDB Goes to the Playground

Believe it or not, I went to the playground today! Mom Pond is making breakfast, and I can smell eggs, toast, and whiffs of coffee, hot chocolate, and tea. Dad Pond gulps down his breakfast and, after he hugs and kisses his family, leaves for work. Mom works part time from home some days, so I am left hanging in her handbag on the banister. The baby is fussing, and little Mary is whining, so she decides to take us for a walk outdoors. She puts her wallet in her fanny pack and holds Mary's hand while pushing the baby stroller. It is a beautiful day with bright sunshine and a gentle breeze.

Mary skips along and stops often to pick flowers for her Mom. I hear a lot of noise as we approach the park. It sounds like children calling out happily to each other. Mom places the baby in a swing with a baby seat while helping Mary onto a swing next to it. With a gentle push, Mary is swinging high. Mom 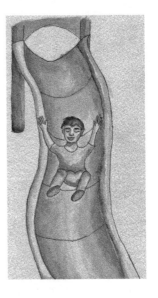 is happily singing "London Bridge Is Falling Down" while gently swinging the baby. She then picks up the baby, who promptly falls asleep in the stroller.

Mary calls out excitedly to her friend, John, and the two of them race to the slides. Children are waiting for their turn to climb up and slide down. Suddenly, a big kid pushes the little children aside, climbs the stairs two at a time, and slides down. He keeps repeating this over and over again to make sure the little ones do not get a turn. That is being mean and now, the children younger than Mary are whimpering because everyone is afraid of the bully. John decides to teach him a lesson. However, Mary cautions him against a fist fight. She is afraid John will get hurt as the bully is so much larger in size.

John whistles and his dog, Rover comes pounding immediately as if from nowhere. John points out the bully, and the dog barks and runs towards the bully. It turns out the bully is terrified of dogs because he was attacked by one as an infant. He tries to run as the dog chases him around the playground. The chase is quite a sight. The bully trips on a stump and falls. He screams. Rover is almost on top of him. John and Mary immediately arrive and command Rover to sit down quietly. Rover does whatever John wants because they are great buddies. Seeing the gentle, loyal dog, the bully feels guilty and is sorry for his actions. He gets up and apologizes.

John explains that Rover is a gentle dog whose bark is worse than his bite. The boy shakes John's and Mary's hands and introduces himself as Henry. John takes Henry's hand and asks him to shake Rover's paw, too. Hesitantly, Henry works up the courage to pet Rover and give him a good scratch behind the ears. With his tail wagging violently, Rover then rolls over, looking for a belly rub.

The little children run over to play Frisbee. Naughty Rover catches the Frisbee and runs away with it, followed by his posse of children. The scene looks like the Pied Piper of Hamelin and the rats! Have you read the fairy tale? If you have not, you must borrow the book from the library and read it. I had a lot of fun learning how the Pied Piper gets rid of all the rats in the town of Hamelin. You see, my previous owners often read this story to the children at bedtime.

Mary and John decide to go on the monkey bars and then convince Mom to join them on the merry-go-round. That is so much fun, being tossed from one side to the other with a big whoosh of wind each time it goes around. You should try it, too! I did not want it to stop! However, I must admit the speed is making me dizzy. It finally slows, and we all get off. Mary and John are slowing down and showing signs of tiredness. Suddenly, peanut butter sandwiches and cut watermelon appear. Henry is delighted to be invited to share this picnic. He can hardly stay away from his newfound friend, Rover. He feels part of a newly acquired family, so he becomes protective of Mary and John.

Meanwhile, they run out of water bottles. Henry volunteers to buy some. Mom goes through her wallet, searching for a $5 bill. While she's holding us, I get to taste peanut butter and the watermelon. Now, I feel I have been a part of the picnic, too. Of course, I get sticky, but I'm not complaining one little bit. With so much gooey stuff, I must have gained weight, as I am having a hard time making room for the other notes.

It is soon time to leave the park. With the promise of another play date, we part with our company and return home. I learned that big and scary-looking kids are not necessarily bullies. They are rather nice if treated with respect. I am not going to label people any more, especially not just after looking at them. Looks can be rather deceiving. I guess that's why they say, "Never judge a book by its cover." I am quite ready for a nap. Until our next outing, then.

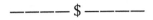

Activities

1. Are the monkey bars or the swings your favorite at the playground? If not, what do you run to first?

2. Always let younger children have a turn on the playground equipment before you. Try not to push anyone. Make a new friend the next time you go to the playground.

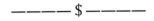

UDB Understands April Fool's Day

I don't understand how my friends born (printed) in April are fools. How do they become fools for just one day? Billie May (BM), the wise one, explains to August Bill (AB) and me, UDB (not Upper Deck Ball, or Umbrella Dumping Bingo, or Upper Descending Balloon, but Unique Dollar Billy) that today is the first of April, and on this day, we play pranks on our friends and teachers. It is called April Fool's Day. We, the Three Billeteers, excitedly scheme and plan to play tricks on Mother March (MoMa) and the other $10 and $20 dollar bills in the wallet.

We scrunch up to become tiny balls and hide ourselves in the inner compartment of the wallet. When Mom Pond looks  for small bills, she cannot find us and is forced to use her coins. Good riddance—they are such noisy coins. MoMa and her friends are very sure we are somewhere but cannot see us. She is always worried that we may fall out in our excitement. Slowly, we stretch and shout "April Fool's!" at the same time. MoMa's worried face turns to a relieved smile and she is truly amused this time.

After yesterday's big family shopping spree that included John, Mary Pond finds John's new shoes at her house. She decides to play a trick on John. She calls and reminds him to come over. He runs over with Rover, his dog, and excitedly puts on his new shoes. While Mary and Rover happily play Frisbee in the yard, John is limping. He cannot understand how his shoes, which were a perfect fit yesterday, are so uncomfortable today. He sits down to remove his shoes, and Rover starts pulling at them. During the ensuing tug of war, Mary shouts, "April Fool!" as that shredded paper stuffing that she put in them earlier falls out. No wonder John's feet did not fit in his new shoes! John laughs good-naturedly and now joins the Frisbee game with enthusiasm.

After Mom's appointment at the hairdresser's, Dad Pond picks her up. She looks transformed. Her hair has red, yellow, and green stripes. She kisses Dad, asking him if he likes her new hairdo. This seems like a trick question. Saying no may result in him getting in trouble and sleeping on the couch tonight, so he says yes, she looks beautiful. Immediately, she rips off the ugly wig, saying, "April Fool's!" Her real hair is nicely curled.

Dad also has a trick up his sleeve! He has brought home Mom's favorite Italian food for dinner. However, she is disappointed when she sees the Chinese carry-out cartons because she is not fond of Chinese food. She opens up the cartons while Dad says, "April Fool's!" The food inside is all Italian. Never judge a book by its cover—always read them. In this case, taste and look at them first.

Mary has invited John to dinner because they have planned to trick her parents. The children offer Mom and Dad a gift box that has two smaller boxes in another, bigger box. Finally, after opening box after empty box, the parents find two pieces of candy wrapped like toffees. They thank the children and put the candies in their mouths. The children shout, "April Fool's!" They have cut and wrapped soap pieces in the candy wrappers. It is a funny sight to see the two parents rush to the bathroom to spit out their "candy" while foaming at the mouth. Though they are both mildly upset, they cannot help laughing.

John still has to trick Mary. As Mary jumps up from her dining chair, John exclaims that Mary has laid an egg. There lies a table tennis ball under her. John has placed the ball there without her knowledge. He finally gets his chance, too. Everyone is laughing and having a good time.

Have you tried playing a prank on anyone? It is fun as long as it is done in a humorous light-hearted way and is not hurtful. Until next April first.

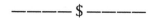

Questions

1. Does April first fall on a Saturday or Sunday this year? Is it a holiday, or do you need to attend school that day?

2. What trick are you planning to play on your best friend? Before you play it, make sure it's a safe and fun trick!

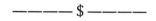

- 8 -

UDB Goes to the Fair

Going to the fair is always so exciting! My friends, BM (not Butchering Musket, but Billie May), AB (not Absolutely Bad, but August Bill), and I (you know me: UDB, not Upset Demented Boy, but Unique Dollar Billy) have gone to fairs before. In fact, the gooey mark I have on George's cheek was caused by the pink cotton candy from last year. However, this year will be my first with this family. I have also heard that the twenty-fifth anniversary of the local fair is going to be extra special this year. We can hardly contain our excitement, which we openly display. There's plenty of crackling, squashing, and stretching of bills in the wallet.

After buying entry tickets, Mom Pond uses her $20 bills to buy coupons for all the rides, games, and food. Being more experienced, the $20 bills taught us a lot—especially Mother March (MoMa), who trained us to be respectful of our neighbors. I will miss them, but I have realized that we may meet again through our lives' journeys. You never know! BM says that I am becoming "philosophical" with age. I don't know what that big word means. It must mean I am becoming more soiled with age, I guess. Fortunately, BM comes to my rescue. She reassures me that I have become calmer and more accepting. Becoming more philosophical with age must mean growing older with more patience. I feel proud then. Maybe I will be like MoMa one day and help the younger ones grow philosophical and age gracefully. However, that seems rather impossible to me, right now.

Children and teenagers are running wild, unable to decide what to do first. Music is blaring through the speakers, the bright lights on all the rides are flashing, and everyone has come to have fun. Mom takes us to the rides first: the carousel for the baby with Dad Pond and the higher-flying merry-go-round for Mom, daughter Mary, and her friend, John. It is so refreshing to feel the cool breeze. We move on to the teacups that swish around and do half and full turns. I can now see how an overfilled cup will run over. Mary and John try the children's roller coaster. However, the teens are screaming on the larger, loopier one. I will admit, I am scared to go on that one. Call me a coward, if you wish.

We need to catch our breath, so games are next on the agenda. Dad throws a perfect basket on his third try in the ball toss booth. His prize is a gorilla stuffed animal. Although this is a good thing, he is stuck carrying the huge fellow around! The children race to the tempting Ferris wheel. It has its own music, and colorful lights rotate with the wheel. The wheel stalls while loading passengers so we are stuck up high for a long time. Off we go with Dad, Mary and John in the waiting carriage, leaving mom and the baby on the ground. The wheel picks up speed, and as we reach

the top, it shudders momentarily and then totally stops. The carriages sway back and forth, and we are scared to move in case we fall. After what seems like an eternity, we are informed that there has been a problem with the wheel. Will we be stuck in the heavens for hours or many days until the problem gets fixed? What happens if it rains? Meanwhile, Mr. Gorilla is dangerously half-hanging from the carriage. The crowds from the fairgrounds that gather beneath us look up helplessly. They are probably thinking a real gorilla's enormous weight has hijacked our ride! The people below look like teeny-weeny ants scurrying around busily. Just then, Mr. Gorilla falls head down and creates a panic situation down there. The ants scream and run wildly.

Soon we hear fire engines. This is getting scary. However, it turns out to be good news. The firemen stretch steep ladders and rescue us one carriage at a time. Being the topmost, we are last. We return to earth from the heavens to tremendous applause—a "standing" ovation since everyone is standing, heads tilted upwards to follow the carriage as it drops down to land safely on the ground. Surprisingly, no one cried or panicked while on the Ferris wheel. I am so proud of Mary, John, and the other children. When everyone remains calm, a rescue party can function quickly and correctly.

The balloon man who comes to cheer us up is so talented. He makes all sorts of shapes by twisting and turning the balloons. Mary wears a blue balloon crown, while John chooses a twisted tie.

We then visit the horrific magical chamber. It is dark and ghostly inside the tent. The magical mirrors make us look thin, tall, fat, thin, and totally crazy. It is fun to scare my friends by making cross-eyed, one-toothed, enlarged faces. AB's spectacles are blown out of proportion, and the Three Billeteers have a good laugh at his expense.

What is a fair without eating cotton candy, roasted corn dipped in butter, funnel cake, and—of course—curly fries? Billie May's necklace is smeared with blue cotton candy. August has powdered sugar all over him, and my blackened eye is stained with butter. Have you noticed that when you get hurt, you tend to keep hurting the same wound again and again? It's like the saying, "adding insult to injury." That's probably how my George feels. Mind you, I'm not complaining.

Now for the best part. It is getting dark, and the laser show starts. We watch spellbound as the lasers dance with the fountains. It is indeed beautiful, but as they say, "All good things must come to an end." Gosh, what an exciting and adventurous day this has been. Without second thoughts, I would definitely repeat it year after year, even if I have to hang upside down! Next time, I should somehow make sure that Mom buys ribbons for Mary and the baby.

You should visit your local fair. BM and AB got to pet some animals at fairs they visited last year. Have a great Fair Day

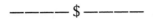

Activities

1. What do you like to do at the fair? Make a list for next year.

2. What color cotton candy do you like best? Draw a picture of yourself eating it.

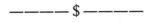

9

"Lucky" UDB Visits the Shopping Mall

There is a tradition in some cultures to request an elder to put a lucky charm in a new wallet. This is to seek the blessings of the goddess of wealth. The wallet can then be used with good fortune. Guess what? I happen to be the first dollar in Mom Pond's wallet. Mom's mother gifted me to her. Until Mom buys a new wallet, I will be traveling around with her. So far, I have been lucky to have Billie May, or should I say Giggly May, and August Bill, the bespectacled dollar bill, on my last few adventures. Every blemish or mark on us (call it dirt, if you want) reminds us of past experiences. They are what makes us who we are. Although we are clones of each other (having been printed at the mint together), we each preserve our individual identities through our distinguishing marks.

Mom decides to go shopping at the mall today. To get there, you must first cross the road. After seating baby Cecily in the stroller, she holds on to daughter Mary in one hand and pushes the stroller with the other. She presses a button, so she receives a signal to teach them to get through the intersection. The flashing, white walking figure is the safe signal. Many pedestrians cross with us. A man in a motorized wheelchair also crosses with great speed. He must be good with his vehicle.

It is a bit chilly in the mall when we get there. The noise, loud music, high ceilings, kiosks in the endless corridors, huge TV screens, and bright lights make it a real outing. Smartly, Mom stops at a kiosk and rents a two-seater Girl Mobile for the children. Mom places her bag in the Mobile, so I get to enjoy the joy ride too. Pushing us through the main corridor, she points out the decorations.

I peek out to see a giant Easter Bunny. Children are being photographed seated on his lap. Baby Cecily wails while she is seated. Fortunately, big sister Mary quickly distracts her with a huge colorful lollipop and poses with her sister and the Bunny for the photograph. From the Bunny's lap, we get to see all kinds of people shop. Some adults are carrying huge shopping bags. Teenagers wearing short shorts are jabbering away while riding the escalators. I see a group of men wearing good walking shoes. Maybe they exercise during lunchtime. It is fun to see how some shoppers are so intense, while others are window shopping ever so leisurely.

As we move along, I see the decorators at a window display setting up their mannequins. This is so interesting, and we stop to watch. The decorator is almost done dressing them in beautiful bridal dresses. As she steps back to arrange their positions, the tallest one accidentally falls and starts a cascade, like dominoes. The mannequin closest to her is about to fall on her. Suddenly, almost out of nowhere, a young man jumps forward and pulls her to safety. With his other hand, he holds on to the closest mannequin and stops the fall. The mall cop rushes to make sure no one is hurt. All is well and everyone is safe.

We move on to do some serious shopping for Easter shoes for Mary. At one store on the ground floor, she finds the ideal size but almost throws a tantrum, as she wants them to be pink and not white. Mom examines the directory that says "You Are Here" with an arrow. What does that mean? Duh, dear sign, I know I am at the mall and I am "here" and not "there." With her finger pressed on the arrow, she figures out the locations of the other shoe stores, and we proceed. Off we go to the second floor.

Mary finds pink shoes, but they are too small for her feet. Oh dear, this is never ending. Two stores later we find that her style is not available. Ready to give up, we move toward an exit, now dragging a whining Mary, when we see her shoes calling us from the display of a ground floor store. We rush in. The saleswoman is extremely helpful. She understands exactly what Mary wants. In a jiffy, she is back, and Mary tries on the new pink pair. She breaks into a smile, and the shoes are bought and packed for her.

We stop for a brief snack break at the eatery. Mary insists on chocolate freeze-dried ice cream that comes in little pellets (Dippin' Dots). While paying for it, one pellet gets stuck on Billie May's throat (her George Washington's throat). Unlike me, she is a chocoholic, so she happily savors it. Like she needs more sugar, hyper as she is! Before I could blink my good eye, unbeknownst to Mom, the baby has yanked and dropped Mary's ice cream on the floor. At the same time, John, who is running toward his friend Mary, slips on it and slides into Mary. Whoa! The two of them crash into three more children in the food line. It looks like a human toboggan (a long sled). They finally stop: two under chairs and three under a table.

There is a moment's silence as everyone is in shock. Suddenly, one child watching this drama unfold bursts out laughing. Soon everyone is roaring with laughter. The laughter is infectious, and it spreads around the room quickly. As the noise subsides, the children get up, and the cleaners run in with their mops before another accident occurs. The ice cream store gives all five fallen children free ice cream for giving them such good publicity.

After finishing our ice cream, we find ourselves in front of the Dance Along screen. It tells us to imitate the moves as it calls out the cues. Oh, this is so much fun. Mom, Mary, John, and even the little baby fall into the rhythm and dance freely, with swaying arms and legs. What a great shopping stress reliever!

After we get home, Mary tries on her shoes and refuses to remove them even at bed time. After she is asleep, Mom manages to remove them slowly and save them for Easter. Shopping can be quite a tiring experience. However, I enjoy the exercise, be it walking around or dancing with the TV. I look around and find that both Billie May and August are also tired and fast asleep. Goodnight!

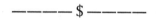

Questions

1. Do you like to go shopping with your parents to the mall? Do they buy you cool shoes and clothes there?

2. What's your favorite store at the mall? What do you like to eat in the mall's food court?

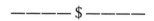

10

UDB Goes Raking Away

In the wallet of Mom Pond, I am cooped up with my elders ($20 bills), Mother March (MoMa) and Grandpa January (GaJa), and my best friends, the other two Billeteers. In case you don't remember, my two friends AB (not Almighty Body, but August Bill) and BM (not Blistering Mouth, but Billie May) and I, UDB (not Ultimately Damaged Book but Unique Dollar Billy) make up the Three Billeteers. MoMa disciplines us, and we learn to respect the elders.

She insists that we are a rowdy bunch, although I have seen her laughing silently at our pranks.

I hear the family say it is fall. I wonder what that means? I did not feel or see our owner fall or get hurt. We travel outside with small and big rakes. Oh, now I get it. It is the time of year when leaves take over our lives. So fall must mean falling leaves. That's good enough for me, as long as no one gets hurt falling. The wallet is removed from the pocket and placed on the doorstep. It flies open, and we stretch out like you cannot imagine. I feel like an open book. Mmm, that feels so good. No more scrunching. We do make a lot of noise, but MoMa does not mind, as it is very noisy outside the house with the breeze and falling leaves.

Squirrels seem to be overloading their storage bins. They're scurrying around with nuts in their mouths and jumping between tree limbs, causing more leaves to fall, as if there weren't enough on the ground already. The birds continue to chirp away.

We peek out and find the whole yard covered with leaves. Our owners start raking, and we hear a lot of scratching noises. Ouch, that must hurt the grass.

Apparently not. The grass is relieved to be able to grow upwards without the leaves blocking them from the sun hovering over them. The children try to help with the raking, but Mary and her friend, John, are having more fun running around the yard. It takes a while before we see mounds of dry leaves.

Suddenly, John's dog, Rover, comes galloping into the yard and jumps on one of the piles. Mary, John, and even baby Cecily follow suit  and laugh as they jump up and down. There are a lot of crackling noises as leaves are crushed beneath their shoes. I guess it does not hurt the poor leaves, as they are dry and have willingly fallen from the trees. Finally, the children fall on one of the biggest mounds, exhausted. The adults are exasperated, but they remember their childhood days, when they used to do the same thing. They smile at each other and, while scooping the children from the leaves, they find themselves being pulled down. They, too, fall on the heap. This is so much fun to watch. I wish I could also jump up and down on the leaves, or even get a bird's-eye view of this beautiful picture. Sometimes, wishes do come true!

I have pushed my friends down and am peeking out so hard that half of me is exposed from the wallet. Just then the breeze turns to a gust of strong wind, and I am blown out of the wallet. *Whoopee!* I am flying away, high towards the sky. Looking around, I find all the trees have become colorful. Beautiful shades of orange, yellow, brown, and even red. I wonder how that happened. It feels like Mother Nature has carefully painted the whole landscape. I am loving this trip on my own.

My owners notice my flight and run to catch me. This is so much fun! Mom runs to secure the rest of the bills in the wallet. Sorry everyone, but this is too much freedom to give up. I will let you know about this adventure if they ever catch me. I fly high but find myself caught in a tree branch. A squirrel runs past me slightly, tearing an edge and dismantling me. I start to fall as Rover catches me. *Eeew!* His saliva is sticky. Another gust of wind makes leaves fly all over the yard. One sticks to me. I say hi to the red leaf but get no response. I figure leaf language must be different from our bill language.

The blowing breeze frees the leaf from me and I find myself in the middle of a huge pile of leaves. Mary picks me up lightly to show her Mom, but with help from gusts of wind, I fly away to the next pile. The whole family is now running after me from pile to pile. It is exhilarating playing hide and seek. Finally, Mary manages to clutch me tightly, and we jump up and down on an untouched mound. With her hands in the air, she lands on her back. Mom comes running to get me, and she too falls on the pile. Everyone is laughing. They are not upset to find their yard looking as though it hadn't been raked at all. Oh well, they will have to seriously rake another day. Finally, I get it. Fall means falling on raked piles.

This has been a fun but exhausting day. I am so excited to share my experiences with my friends. However, once I am placed safely in the wallet, I fall asleep. I suppose this is my body's response, as it is not used to so much freedom. As they say, "all good things must come to an end."

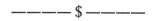

Questions and Activities

1. Have you ever tried hiding under a pile of raked leaves before? Is it like playing hide and seek?

2. Make a collection of different colored leaves for show-and-tell in class.

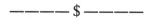

- 11 -

UDB Rides the Garbage Truck

Many mornings, we, the Three Billeteers, have been rudely awakened by the sound of a truck that stops and starts outside the house and goes up and down the street doing the same. I never knew what kind of truck it was until the day we actually rode in one.

Billie May (BM), August Bill (AB) and I, UDB (again, I am not Under Developed Belly or Upper Dangling Buffoon, but Unique Dollar Billy) are peacefully sleeping in the wallet of Mom Pond's handbag, which is hanging on the baby's stroller. Baby Cecily decides to take the stroller on a trip through the kitchen when the handbag gets caught in one of the tires. Ouch, that hurts! We are squashed and all crumpled up as she tries to run over the bag. Highly frustrated by now, she lifts and drops the bag in the garbage bin. Later, Mom ties up the garbage and puts the bin out at the curb with her handbag! Oh no!

I later learn that the noisy truck is the garbage collection truck. The garbage man lifts the bin onto some kind of machine that lifts us up high. This is fun until he dumps us into a huge heap of messy garbage. My stomach is lurching by this time. It feels like the high drop on a rollercoaster! We are quite alone in the handbag and in the middle of an enormous amount of smelly rubbish. Suddenly, another machine starts, and we move around and around. This is fun until we are further embedded among rotting food. Phew, what an awful stink! The truck is now on its way to the neighbor's house.

Being a restless spirit, I start to squirm. I am warned by wise BM that it is best not to move. Hopefully, a rescue squad will take us back to Mom soon. Of course, I don't believe BM, so I decide to snoop around a bit. As I peek out, I find the smell unbearable. But the smell isn't the worst part—it even looks nasty! Everything is mushed together and looks awful. All the paper is wet and listless. Cut fruit has lost its shape. A rotten tomato washes by me—or is it watermelon? It is difficult to tell. Suddenly, the truck jerks, and a splotch of red something falls on my United States seal. I hope my George Washington is spared this time. Oh dear, whatever it is smells terrible, and I find that the red soiling watermark is traveling through me. George might actually come out of this wearing a red rose, but definitely not smelling like one. I pinch myself, hoping this is only a bad dream. Unfortunately, this is reality. No kidding.

This is like adding insult to injury. George now looks like he has scarlet fever. Poor guy. I hope Bill's

Cleaners will be able to get me cleaned when I get out of this trash hole. I jump back into the wallet and decide to wait it out. BM and AB don't want to be anywhere near me, as I am very dirty by now and smell absolutely terrible. BM tells us that we might find ourselves under a mountain of trash in the main dump, and a look of horror spreads across my face. Now I am really scared.

At the neighbor's house, the garbage man empties out their trash bin into our dump and starts the machine that churns us. Ouch, ouch, we are really squashed now, as the handbag is flattening. Suddenly, the garbage man stops the rotation (which, incidentally, is no longer fun) as he notices something shining in the garbage. It turns out to be the shiny chain attached to the handle of the handbag. With gloved hands, he picks out the handbag. Phew, what a soggy mess. He dries it out on his seat, finds Mom's ID in it, and decides to walk it over to our home.

When Mom opens the door, the garbage man is surprised to find the house looking like a tornado has hit it. Drawers and cupboards are open, and laundry

is strewn over the couch.
Things on the table are
upturned. Mom has franti-
cally been looking for her
handbag and was about to
make some calls when we
arrived. With a smile, the
garbage man holds out her

bag. Profusely thanking him, she kisses it and instantly
screws up her nose, as the smell is unbearable.
However, she is still very happy to have us back.

Mary comes crying to Mom, confessing it is all
her fault. She had seen Cecily walking the stroller
but did not think she would throw the handbag into
the garbage can. She did not want to tattle and was
ready for her punishment. Mom hugs her two children tightly and definitely does not punish them. She
realizes she needs to keep important things beyond
the baby's reach. Mary is such a responsible, mature
older sibling who always looks out for her younger
sister. I am so proud of her.

I too learned an important lesson that day. It does not pay to be too snoopy. As they say, "curiosity kills the cat!" Nobody wants to be anywhere near me right now with my RED seal, my George in red/pink clothes, and my awful stink! Mom is already removing us one by one and laying us out to dry while getting ready to wash out her handbag. I realize I am going to need severe deep cleaning. Now that I am home, I feel safe, and that is all that matters to me. No more rides in the garbage truck for me! But it was worth exploring this one time.

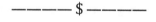

Questions/Activities

1. Would you like to ride beside the driver on a garbage truck?

2. Always remind your parents to keep things beyond your little sister's or little brother's reach so they don't get into mischief.

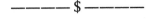

- 12 -

UDB Goes to the Ballpark

While visiting relatives in another state, I heard Dad Pond talk about going to a baseball game this season. He informs us that he has bought tickets for this Saturday's game at the ballpark. Having used up his cash to buy tickets, he is forced to borrow money from Mom Pond. This turns out to be our lucky day! We get transferred to

Dad's wallet. We are so excited that he is taking Mary and her cousin, Mike, to the game and, naturally, us Billeteers too. In case you do not know us, we are BM (not Bubbling Mess, but the all-knowing "Billie May"; AB (not Apple Blintz, but my buddy, "August Bill") and myself, UDB (not United Deposit Bank, but "Unique Dollar Billy").

We are going to a double header. Now, what is a double header? Does that mean they will chop off two heads? Not in this day and age, I hope. Actually, it is two games that are one after another and between the same teams. The children are excited, and so are we. This is our first ball game, so we are hyper and cannot seem to sit quiet. Mike takes his baseball glove along. I cannot understand why he only has one glove. He is also wearing his cap backwards. "Looks cool!" says Mary. Mom slathers Mary with a whole lot of sunscreen to make sure that she doesn't get sunburn. She, too, wears a baseball cap and is ready. Dad makes sure he has his cap, his wallet, and money (which includes us).

We get to the ballpark. A huge host of parking attendants with cool, neon, lighted batons guides us to our parking aisles and spots. Dad writes down the aisle and spot numbers because he has been known to get lost looking for his car after a game. Before entering the stadium, we must be screened through X-ray machines. They say this is for security reasons. Fortunately, we bills in the wallet do not need to worry; it doesn't hurt us. We have to walk in long circles around the stadium to get to our entrance. It seems like it is on the other side of the Earth! An usher points us to our seats. Finally, when we reach our seats and can't contain ourselves any longer, we peek out.

We see a nicely manicured green diamond with a mud mound in the middle and four small mounds at the corners. Apparently, these are the pitcher's mound and the four bases. To help us see the game better, there are many TV monitors hung around us. The scores are exhibited on huge monitors for all to see on all sides of the diamond. There are also lots of flashing advertisements displayed on the fences surrounding the field. I find them a bit disturbing, but I guess the income from them is what keeps the games alive. We'll just have to deal with it and learn to ignore it.

Suddenly, an organ plays loudly over the speakers, and the start of the game is announced by introducing the home team and the opponents. I see the players come out from a "dugout." Why would players need to dig themselves out of a hole to play ball? They face each other in two lines. They run through, high-fiving their teammates. I think they should high-five their opponents too. After the national anthem is sung beautifully by a teenager in a wheelchair, the captains shake hands, and the opposing team bats first with the home team pitching. Needless to mention, the home team gets the loudest and longest cheers.

The pitcher, who is allowed seven warm-up throws, first practices with his catcher, who wears a face guard. His throws look stronger than the kind used to throw balls for dogs to chase. "Well, duh!" says BM! The rest of the team throws warm-up balls to each other, and finally the ball does a round from one baseman to another and ends up in the hands of the pitcher. I now see that all the players are wearing only one glove each. I am told by AB that they wear their glove on their best catching hand. It depends on whether they are right- or left-handed. I get it now! They have to make one-handed catches—how difficult!

Meanwhile, the batsmen are warming up, too, by doing silly dance moves with their bodies and turning from side to side with heavy bats. They wear helmets that cover only the ear that faces the pitcher so they do not get hurt. Don't you think that covering only one ear feels like one lost earring? Maybe—BM would know more about this. The batsman then takes position facing the pitcher with the catcher and the umpire behind him. The pitcher twists his body into weird shapes and throws the ball at top speed. The ball is pitched very, very fast. Maybe at 100 miles per hour? To me, it is almost at the speed of light—although I don't know how fast that is.

I learn that the game is about a batsman scoring a run, which includes touching all four bases or hitting a "home run" that is high over the fence of the ball field. If the ball is pitched at top speed at a precise angle that the batsman is unable to hit, that ball is called a "strike." Each batsman is allowed three "strikes" before he "strikes out." The batsman is not out when foul non-strikes or four "balls" are pitched. He then gets to walk to first base.

Now, let's get back to the action on the field. The first pitch is a "ball." The next one is a "foul," as it hits the batsman's wood bat and goes high into the stadium above his head. Fans rush to catch the ball. Aha! Now I understand why boys bring their gloves—obviously to catch these fly balls. These balls must be precious. Children rush to have them autographed by the players at the end of the game. As I am wishing one fly ball would come our way, the foul ball soars toward us. Dad jumps high, catches it, and places it in Mike's glove. You should have seen the joy on Mary and Mike's faces. It was like they had caught the ball themselves!

You can now hear and see the crowds showing their support for the players. This is most enjoyable. The organ plays a popular, catchy tune. The home fans start banging their feet and clap in unison until I hear the word "Charge" at the end. This must really boost the players' confidence. As if practiced in advance, the crowds stand and form a "wave," row by row. Oh, so cool! A human wave is formed by fans standing in turn and raising and waving their arms from side to side.

I hear that the home team is called "The Brewers." BM tells me that we must be at the Miller Park Stadium in Milwaukee, Wisconsin, also known as America's Dairyland. The opponents are the Nationals from Washington, DC. I wonder which team I should root for. I realize it does not truly matter because the best team should win.

At the bottom of the next inning, the Brewers are batting with a batsman who runs to first base. The second batsman hits a Home Run. *Whoopee!* The organ plays "Roll Out the Barrel," and a guy slides into the beer barrel on the scoreboard. Huge beer bubbles come out of the barrel. Oh my, so much excitement! The crowds are cheering loudly. At the next pitch, crowds "boo" the opponents. Now, I don't think that is right; everyone should be given a fair chance. I guess the Brewers get treated the same way at games away from their home stadium. In my opinion, that still does not make it right.

While the game continues, I experience another delightful part of baseball. I am talking about the fast food sold by vendors loudly calling out their eats and drinks. Here comes the lemonade and beer man. A guy in the center orders a beer. The vendor opens a foaming bottle and pours it into a cup. By the time it changes so many hands and reaches him, half the beer has fallen on jeans, T-shirts, and on the ground.

Dad gets popcorn and lemonade for the children and us. The same man in the center orders popcorn, too. I am going to call him CF (Center Fan). This time, it passes through at least ten pairs of hands. When it reaches Mike, the gloved hand tips it slightly over Mary's head by mistake. Mary looks like she is wearing a white crown, like a Baseball Princess. Mike quickly helps himself to a handful of popcorn. The remaining popcorn looks like flowers in Mary's hair and cap! Again, CF gets only a quarter of his share. It's not fun sitting in the center if you plan to order food from the aisles! Roasted peanuts in cones get shelled and thrown on the floor. I feel guilty about littering. I hear it is a custom that's allowed only at the stadium. I am stuffed by now, as the wallet has been opened and closed many times, and I have tasted all the food the children ordered. It's a good thing Mom gave Dad lots of $10 and $20 bills so we don't get traded.

At the seventh inning, everyone takes a short break, including the players and crowds. I believe this is called the seventh inning stretch. Everybody is on their feet to stretch. Yes, it does feel good to stretch after all this jumping up and down, cheering, screaming, eating, and drinking. All the bills are stretching and settling in to watch the final innings.

The game must be decisive, so it can have more than the usual nine innings. Suddenly, I hear, "It's a steal!" I don't see a thief running away with the solid concrete base. A batsman runs to first base and slides— almost swims—to second base without being caught. This must be a "steal." The score is tied 7 to 7, and now the Brewers get to bat at the bottom of the ninth inning. Three balls and two strikes have been pitched, and all the bases are loaded. This is tense, and there is a hush in the stadium.

The Brewer batsman hits hard, and it's a *home run!* The game is won by the Brewers. A home run does not mean you have to run all the way home! It means the batsman hits the ball over the fence of the ball field and scores. All the runners get to run through all the bases to fourth base, and in the process, they make so many runs. Plenty of high fives are exchanged with the winning team running into the ball field now. The organ plays, the crowds cheer and clap, and the bubbles rise high from the barrel. The Goodyear blimp in the sky releases balloons and confetti in the sky. Fans are covered with confetti and catching the balloons landing near them. I hear fireworks, too. That's a lot of sound and light! Wow, what a celebration! This is so much fun.

We are so tired that we leave. In fact, no one minds missing the next game. This game had such an exciting finish. Dad buys new caps for the children on the way out. This time, he manages to find the parked car. The children are asleep in their car seats even before we leave the parking lot. I look around and find BM and

AB are also asleep. The older bills are already snoring—just from watching the game?

Have you gone to a baseball game before? One of these days, you should go to a game at the Brewer stadium just to watch the scoreboard!

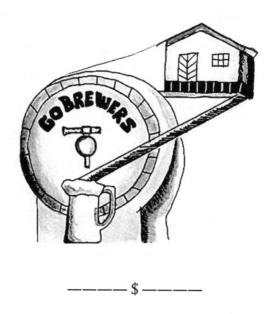

————— $ —————

Activities

1. The next time you are at the ballpark, try starting
    a wave, especially when your team is winning.

2. Ask your parents if you could meet the players
    during some game to get their autographs on
    your baseball glove.

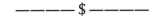

- 13 -

UDB Goes Grocery Shopping

It is grocery shopping day, and Mom Pond has her list, coupons, and bags ready. She asks Dad Pond for money, and that is how we $1 bills find ourselves back in Mom's handbag. Grocery shopping can be fun, but exhausting, too. There is too much brain power required. You might wonder why. Well, you first have to find the product in the correct aisle. Then, there are too many choices that need to be narrowed down. There are too many things to calculate, too! Some will show their items as $1.03/lb, while others will show $4.69/item. Then, you have to check how much the item weighs. You have to be sure you choose the best and cheapest product. You have to be a whiz at math to get the best price.

My Billeteer friend, the wise BM (not Bubble Maker, but Billie May) and the nerdy AB with glasses (not Altogether Baloney, but August Bill) are good at this. I, UDB (not Usher Duty Boy, but Unique Dollar Billy) am the lazy one and feel my owners know best. So far I have been tucked away in Mom's wallet, so I have not made an effort. One of these days, I am sure I will get traded and have a rude awakening. I have made up my mind. Today I will try to do the math.

Mom puts Mary and baby Cecily in the car and we are off to the local grocery store. Baby Cecily is excited to see the little yellow car in front of the grocery cart. However, she is fussing and whining today. I am convinced she must be teething, as she is trying to bite into everything she can lay her hands on. When baby teeth or milk teeth start growing, babies feel a lot of pain. I know all about this because I have been around so many cranky babies before. Mom puts Cecily in the grocery cart so that Cecily is facing her. As we enter, Mary is given a small grocery cart that has a flag that reads, "Customer-in-Training." She is all smiles and proudly pushes it around.

As we go from aisle to aisle, Mom is stooping, bending, and reading the labels on the products. I am sure she is doing the math and examining the items. She does not notice that Cecily has picked up many items at easy reach and dumped them into the cart. Cecily sees Mary's cart is empty, so she hands Mary chocolates and small boxes of sweetened cereal. Meanwhile, Mary is quite happy to fill her cart.

Mom quietens Cecily's whining with a banana. Unknowingly, Cecily throws the peel on the floor. Just then, Mary's friend, John, sees Mary and runs to help her push her cart. He slips and slides towards Mary. Her cart overturns and hits the cereal shelf. Cereal boxes topple from the top shelves. It feels like an earthquake! Items on all the shelves are shaking. Immediately, the manager and store helpers rush to the scene. One carries Mom and Cecily's cart away from the aisle. The other carries Mary and John to the other end of the aisle. The aisle is now full of cereal and boxes that have split open due to the impact. You can hear the Cheerios popping as the helpers step on them. What a mess! The children are laughing at one end, and the manager is unable to keep a stern face.

However, Mom's face is turning red with embarrassment. She profusely apologizes for the chaos. Within minutes, the floor is swept and all is calm again. Mary is handed an empty cart now. She actually doesn't mind, as she is tired of pushing around so much of Cecily's stuff.

Cecily is howling by this time, and it takes all of Mom's energy to calm her down and push her cart around. Store helpers bring lollipops for her and the other children and help to push the cart around. We stop at a corner where a lady is giving out free samples of salsa and tortilla chips. Yummy! I like hot salsa. Hope I get to taste it when the wallet is opened at the checkout counter.

Reusable shopping bags are encouraged nowadays to save the environment, and Mom always has some in the car. She thought she had brought enough, but she finds herself asking for extra reusable store bags. She is also rather surprised to pay a hefty bill this time. When she sees the receipt, she finds items that were not on her list. Dog food (they don't even have a dog!), chocolates, potato chips, chewing gum, and Twinkies have found their way into the cart!

Cecily is totally clueless as she sucks on her lollipop. Mom is thinking ahead and decides to give the dog food to John for his dog, Rover. She will take the other items to the homeless shelter later. Not wanting to create another scene, Mom pays the fat bill. However, she is now short on money. Guess what? We get traded. The Billeteers get pulled out along with some change. Quickly, we say our goodbyes. These separations are natural, and we are sure to meet again. We just don't know when and where. Our $20 MoMa (Mother

March) curls around us with blessings and instructions to be well behaved. Mom is helped with getting the groceries and children loaded into her car.

We are now in the checkout box in neat piles of one, five, ten, and twenty dollar bills. Thank heavens the noisy coins are in another holder. The Three Billeteers are fortunately together in the same pile. Meanwhile, I meet some of my old friends. I have not seen them in a long time. There is so much to talk about as we exchange stories. We don't mind being loud. The rattle of the checkout box being opened and closed is louder than us. We realize that hundreds of customers go grocery shopping every day. I guess everyone has to eat to survive!

Speaking of food, I am hungry. I didn't get enough salsa because BM and AB were on either side of me and have more stains than me. Maybe if I get closer to them, I will be able to smell the salsa at least. I better take a nap now, as we will get transported to the bank tonight to be cleaned at "Bill's Cleaners" as we have named the whirring machine. A whirl in this machine gives us a dry clean, and we come out starched and no longer sticky. Feeling fresh, we are then ready for our next journey. Who knows, the Three Billeteers may still land in the same pile. Goodbye, until we meet again.

————— $ —————

Activities

1. When you run out of cereal, peanut butter, jelly, or bread, add it to the grocery list on the refrigerator door. Remind your parents to take the grocery list to the store.

2. Help your parents put away the groceries when you return home.

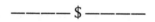

- 14 -

UDB Visits School

My new owners cash a check at the bank and ask for single dollars. I find myself in the handbag of Mom Cherry with the three children: Jim (nine years old), Brian (six), and little Jill (four). Sometimes, they call it a handbag, and sometimes, a purse. They can never make up their minds! I don't blame them. It's just too many choices! In any case, crisp new notes have found their way near me. Oh dear, I am already itching with their starched rustling movements. Hope they will settle down so we can become friends. Let's see who we have here—$5 Nancy September (but she is rightly called Nosy, as you will see later) and $1 SO (Sonny October), a nice fellow. His edges are dog-eared, and every time he laughs, his edges perk up like the ears of a dog! "Dog ears" now make sense to me. Our voluntary supervisor, MoMa ($20 bill, Mother March) has been replaced by wrinkled $20 PoJa (Pops January.) He does not look as strict as MoMa, so I think we will have a good time. Watch out! I may be wrong, as looks can be rather

deceiving, like first impressions.

It is School Visitation Day, when parents get to visit their childrens' classes. Jill is allowed to accompany her mom, so she is super excited. She actually begs to ride the school bus, but I think that is asking for too much. However, Mom allows her to carry her small Cinderella backpack. She now looks like a regular school student scampering all over the house with her backpack and crayons. She is running around, so scampering must mean rushing about and not tricking, as in scam. Also, I don't see how a four-year-old can be a scammer!

Mom Cherry first enters Brian's class, which is filled with proud first graders. Jill and Mom get to sit at the back in little chairs with desks for writing. I feel sorry when a very tall parent (he looks about ten feet tall to me) tries to fit into one of them. Oops! He does not manage, and the chair falls with a tall thud, causing much laughter among the children. He too laughs and decides to stand and observe. The teacher assembles her students around her as they learn the Pledge of Allegiance. Brian is asked to lead the class as they all recite it. Everyone immediately stands with their hands on their hearts, including Jill. That must be so cute—I try peeking above Nosy and SO, but their starched edges are so scratchy. They realize my problem and push me up. Nosy has already peeked high enough to look around. Jill looks adorable standing with her hand on her heart and muttering something to keep pace with Brian and his classmates!

The children form a circle around the teacher and sing their ABCs. Then they move to their respective tables and are given crayons to draw a picture of their favorite sport. The teacher gives Jill a sheet and crayons, too, and seats her beside Brian. While Brian is drawing a baseball field with players, Jill manages a huge, multi-shaped ball. Brian says it looks like a mutilated ball! I figure mutilate must mean disfigure because her ball looks out of shape. However, she may become an artist in the future, the teacher says! Jill is so proud of her work, and she gets to keep the sheet. I bet she thinks if school is all about drawing mutilated balls, then she will ace it!

Next, we go to Jim's fourth grade classroom. Again, we sit patiently on little chairs at the back for longer. This class would like us to sit through two assignments. The teacher first instructs the students to write an essay on what they don't like about school. She looks around the smiling faces and asks if there are any burning questions. This I don't get—"burning" questions? Will smoke come out of their heads? There are lots of sneers in the handbag. PoJa takes control. With a gruff noise, he tells everyone to be quiet. We are now scared of him. PoJa explains that a burning question is a million-dollar question. I wish I could ask such a question so I could win a million dollars. Then again, what would I do with one million of us $1 bills? I can barely take care of myself. Thanks, but no thanks. I am content being UDB.

Fortunately, no one in the class asks a "burning" or "firing" question, so the buzzer goes off for the students to start writing. Jill, meanwhile, draws on her sheet. "Pencils down!" the teacher announces. Jim and his friends read out their complaints—too early to get up, bus is cold, too much homework, bullies in the gym, not enough recess time—oh my, the list goes on! SO tells me that hearing all this, Jill will probably become disillusioned. Now what is that? Maybe Jill is ill—hey, that rhymes—Jill, ill! Jokes apart, SO explains it means she may now realize that school is not all fun, as she has imagined.

The next assignment is announced—now the students need to write about what they like about school. Again, without any burning million-dollar questions, the buzzer sounds. I find that this class is well-disciplined. Students stand and read out their essays only when their names are called. Now, this assignment has many interesting answers. The majority say they like meeting and playing with their friends in school, while others say they like meeting classmates from other countries, learning about different cultures, participating in Talent Day with friends, eating healthy ethnic foods during class parties (instead of the usual cupcakes), helping friends with math and reading, bringing funny stuff for "show and tell," and so on. Most of the answers are centered on playing with buddies and making best friends.

When class is dismissed for lunch, the students line up to go to the cafeteria. Today Jim gets to eat lunch with his Mom, Brian, and Jill. As they buy lunch, Jim helps to carry Jill's tray. Mom tells Jim and Brian how proud of them she is. Jim's friends join the table as they exchange hearty laughs and show how much they like school and being with each other.

Jill insists on getting spaghetti for lunch. Mmmm, smells good! She has this habit of sucking whole strands into her mouth and swallowing them right away. Imagine eating worms without chewing them! Phew! Her mouth is red (she looks like she has red lip gloss on!). Just as she takes another scoop, the plate tilts over and the tray falls on the floor with a huge bang. The children burst into laughter. Mom is embarrassed and rushes to get paper towels. The teachers are smiling—this must be an everyday occurrence for them! Jim asks for more money to buy Jill pudding because she is whining. As usual, $5 Nosy is peeking out. Mom takes Nosy and hands her to Jim. As Jim tries to hurry, he slips and lands on top of the tray. Again there is loud laughter! The children must think this is some kind of a funny family show. It must be so much fun to live in Jim's house!

Meanwhile, Nosy falls right on top of the spilt red sauce. With Nosy out, I have more space to peek out. Haha, she looks crazy. Her back is smeared red. She now has a "Red House," not a White House. Who would believe she had just been to the cleaners! Serves her right for being so nosy! We can't help laughing and stretching. Cleaners mop up the mess, and Mom puts Red Nosy back in her handbag. She decides it is time for Jill's nap, and they leave immediately.

For sure, I don't want to be next to Nosy in case the sauce is still wet and my George Washington gets a Red nose. Again, PoJa gruffly tells us to calm down as he makes Nosy fall in last so she can dry out without smudging us. Although PoJa never raises his voice like the fourth grade teacher, we learn to mind him very quickly. He is very likable, but we know better than to cross him. We are very quiet on the way back.

Jill entertains us. She thinks she is singing the Pledge of Allegiance with her hand on her heart. She is so looking forward to joining her brothers in school. In fact, she becomes jealous every day as they board the bus without her. We tell her, "Just you wait, dear. All in good time."

Mom is pleased with the teachers and the boys' progress. She will have a lot to tell Dad Cherry when he gets home. Off to get Jill into bed for a nap now before she gets too tired. I heard Dad tell Mom that before the weather gets cold, they should take the children for a short break somewhere. I wonder where they plan to go. I am already excited. However, we better settle down and remain quiet before we annoy PoJa.

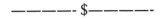

Questions/Activities

1. Do you like having your parents come to your class? Do you like having lunch with them at school?

2. Before the next school visitation day, make something special to share with your parents.

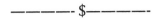

- 15 -

UDB Goes to the Beach

I, UD (Unique Dollar) Billy, am shoved into Mom Cherry's wallet. At first, I am shy, feeling scrunched and self-conscious of my one black-eyed George Washington. However, as soon as I meet up with my old friends, Peter September (PS) and Jenni February (JF), I feel better. I used to call PS "Post Script" because he always thinks of things to say or mention after we had finished our discussion. JF was Jumping Frog, as she is always hyper, with her never-ending questions and chatter. This time I am stuck in between them, so I am resigned to a lot of scratching and whispering.

The Cherry family—the parents, nine-year-old Jim, six-year-old Brian, and four-year-old Jill—decides to go to the beach for a vacation. *Whoopee!* We are so excited that JF nearly jumps out of the wallet. Packing is finished, the van is loaded, seat belts are fastened, and off we go! We have hardly hit the freeway when Jill asks if we are there already. Her drone of "When will we get there?" is never-ending. Fortunately, all three children are tired, and they eventually fall asleep. We arrive at the motel in a few hours, and everyone changes into swimsuits. Mom lathers them with tons of sunscreen lotion. I hear her say that this is to prevent the skin from getting burnt by the sun. When she touches her wallet and the bills in it, we smell the lotion, too. The smell is not intolerable, but it does taste gross!

Even before we arrive at the beach, we can hear the waves and smell the sea. Two long chairs are rented beneath a huge umbrella (for shade, I guess.) I feel Mom hopping on the sand. It must be warm for her bare feet as she opens a bamboo rug for the children and their beach toys.

The children run to the water with their parents running behind them and shouting for them to wait. The waves can be dangerous, so the parents hold Brain and Jill's hands while soaking their feet in the water. Brian is wringing his hands out of Mom's grasp. He cannot understand why Jim is allowed to wade a little further out into the water. He does not notice that Dad is behind Jim, watching him like a hawk. While the sand is warm, the water is cold at their feet. All of them gasp and try to walk backwards as a huge wave comes in. Everyone is told to dig in their heels, but the children are so delighted that they jump when a wave comes in, and especially as it recedes. JF tells us that there is a lot of white foam around and heaps of seaweed on the beach. I peek out now and almost catch a wave to the face. Frightened, I quickly fold inwards. I don't want Mom to get drenched or fall into the water. We will all be reduced to pulp. My special marks may get washed out, and I will totally lose my identity, and probably my shape, too! Although I don't mind getting sticky, I pray that I will retain my identification marks. Needless to say, I have grown fond of them because they remind me of my past experiences! I so want to remain Unique.

Jill constantly follows her older brothers around, and she worships Jim. She watches intently as Jim tries to build a sand castle. She uses her square and triangular scoops to make 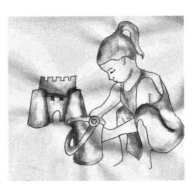 little mounds, too. Jim asks her to fetch wet sand for his castle, and she obediently fills her little plastic buckets many times. Finally, the castle starts taking shape. Brian is a bookworm and has learned a new word today. Watching Jim and Jill play together, he feels dejected and lonely. He runs and tramples over the castle, kicks it, and calls it "hogwash." I wonder what "hogwash" means. Washing a pig, I think. How is a sand castle like washing a pig? I am confused. By this time, Jill is crying loudly and pointing to Brian and the demolished castle, while Jim is ready to beat up Brain. He complains to his father that Brain is using bad language and called his work "hogwash."

First, Mom pacifies Jill and then takes Brain aside to have a talk with him about his bad behavior. Dad, meanwhile, explains to Jim that while Brain's action is inexcusable, *hogwash* is not a bad word. It means *rubbish* or *bunkum* or *humbug*. I understand *garbage*, but like hogwash, I have never heard bunkum and humbug before. As they say, you learn something new every day. I have learned three new words today: hogwash, bunkum, and humbug. I keep repeating, "Bunkum, humbug ... humbug, bunkum," to myself. They do have such a nice ring to them. They even sort of rhyme together. Have you come across rhyming words before? Try repeating them again and again. It is fun!

Mom realizes that Brian is sometimes jealous of his older brother and spoils his Lego structures like he kicked the sand castle. He damages stuff just to get attention. Being a middle child, he feels that he needs to prove himself, as he is constantly compared to his brother and sister. She realizes that she needs to spend time alone with him and make him understand how special he is. He is way ahead of his grade level in reading and math, for example. She understands that she needs to make him feel confident and boost his self-esteem. She decides to take him for ice cream alone while Dad takes the other two to wash up; they have buckets of sand stuck to their clothes.

Although Brian may not agree with me at the moment, being the middle child is not so bad. I am in the middle of my bill buddies, and I kind of like being there. I have friends on either side of me, and they not only protect me, but also peek out and let me know when the coast is clear and it is safe for me to peek, too. They actually look out for me, literally. In any case, what can be better than having ice cream with Mom alone? Yummy! I, too, get to taste one of my favorite flavors, Heavenly Mango Orange, as Mom pays for it. I find that Brian and I have similar tastes. Brian is cuddling with his Mom and feels special and confident already. He runs towards his siblings, allowing them to take a lick of his ice cream.

Back at the motel, everyone takes a shower one by one in the outdoor bathroom to wash off the sand before entering their rooms. The stall seems like fun; you can see the sky above while showering! Vacations can be great fun and exciting. However, they never seem to last long enough. The beds are inviting, and everyone is asleep before you know it. Meanwhile, I am unable to get the new words I learned today out of my head—hogwashing, humbugging and bunkuming—not rubbishing away, mind you. As soon as my mind stops buzzing with these words, I hope to fall asleep.

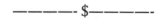

Activities

1. When you are at the beach, keep a journal of the new friends you make. You never know—you might meet them again on your next trip.

2. Help your parents to understand your siblings. After all, everyone is special, but sometimes we do feel hurt and misunderstood.

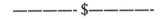

- 16 -

UDB Dances in the Rain?

It is Saturday, and my owners make plans to take the children on an outing. To where, is the question. I would love to know—not that I have a choice, as I will have to go wherever they go. I really don't mind, as I have had so many fun adventures and collected so many marks to remember my experiences. Hopefully, these are marks of maturity! Everyone says I need to grow up. What does that mean? Do

I graduate from being a $1 bill to a $5 bill? I don't want to lose my well-earned marks, and I don't need more hassles. Who wants to behave prim and proper, all starched and stiff? My spots, dirty or colored scratches, blotches, stains, blemishes, or imperfections (depends on how you look at them), make me UDB (not Upset Demented Book, but Unique Dollar Billy.) I have decided to be who I am, my Unique self, and enjoy each day to the fullest. Are you on board? On to our next adventure, then.

I have the big task of waking up my buddies, PS (not Party Supplier, but Peter September) and JF (not Jumbo Fries—though I wish I had some—but Jenni February.) They are rather quiet today in the wallet. Too much partying yesterday, I suppose, although I must admit we were extremely tired. I nudge them, but there is no reaction, so I decide to stretch, making loud, scratching noises and tickling them with my edges. That definitely wakes them up, giggling as they open their eyes. However, the firm $5 next to us gives us a haughty glare, like we are so immature! We smile and entice him to join the fun. I am sure we all have a child within us, and it is good to let go our worries and behave like one every once in a while.

Today is an overcast day. As my owners, the Cherrys, load the car, it starts to drizzle. I can smell the mud as the first drops of rain wet it. Mmmm, I love this smell so much that I actually feel like tasting the mud. Have you ever had a craving to eat something when you like the smell?

Oh no! It is really raining now. No way am I getting wet! Strong gusts of wind rattle the windows. The adults run through the house closing windows, almost stepping on Jim's Lego masterpiece. It is supposed to be the Washington Monument, but it looks more like the Leaning Tower of Pisa. I hope you get to visit these two monuments. They are really worth seeing.

Soon, we hear the pitter-patter of rain on the sunroof. Oh dear! The noise grows louder as it starts to hail. Jim exclaims that he can see hailstones as big as golf balls. Do people play golf with golf stones? I see the hail and realize that hailstones refer to round pieces of ice falling from the skies. I am sure that Jim is exaggerating, as the hail looks more like small marbles to me. Car drivers must be rammed on the roof and windshield of their cars by the hailstones. I hope our car remains undamaged.

I am rather puzzled. Have you ever wondered how ice falls from the skies? I have often wondered how hail falls in *round* pieces and not *square?* I figure it must have started as a *huge* round ball, and by the time it reaches us, it breaks into smaller and smaller pieces and showers down as hailstones.

The children crowd to the front window. Their noses and fingers leave dirty marks on the clean glass. I am sure Mom Cherry and the windows themselves are not happy, but at least it keeps them out of mischief. The rain is relentless, and as the wind props open the front door, the children run out carrying umbrellas. They stomp on the puddles and comment on the water draining from their umbrellas. Jill says the water pouring down from hers is more than Brian's, and this starts a running battle. The umbrellas are discarded, and wet clothes stick to their bodies as they laugh and jump rowdily. They turn their faces to the sky with eyes closed. It must feel so blissful, like a feeling of truly letting go.

Fortunately, even though it is raining, it is a warm day. The two adults look out the window and laugh, seeing their children having so much fun. As Mom stows her wallet on the windowsill, Dad Cherry plays an old record and gently guides Mom outside. They are drenched in minutes, but it doesn't seem to bother them. They are dancing and swirling in the rain! How romantic! The children form a circle around them, and soon the whole family is holding hands, dancing and singing loudly to the music.

I am actually jealous of the children, as I dare not get wet. However, JF, PS, and I are peeking out and swaying to the music playing in the house. The tune is stuck in our heads even after it stops and we carry on. Our edges are waving like little flags. The $5 bill does not wait for an invitation; he joins us cheerfully. We end up having fun in our own way.

Mom brings the troops in wrapped in towels and shivering to have hot chocolate and warm cookies. The rain stops, and everyone is dry. Outside, it appears to be still and quiet with the sun peeking out. It is indeed a lovely time for a leisurely walk, so we go out again.

Birds are chirping, flowering plants are upright, and puddles are drying as the rain water from the roads is washed down to the reservoirs. Even the children walk in silence, awed by the beauty, sounds, and smells of the atmosphere. Walking under trees, you might think it is still raining; drops fall on my owners' heads when the leaves move to and fro. My George Washington does not wear a hat, but if he did, I would tip it to Mother Nature's wonders!

Suddenly, a most beautiful sight appears in the sky: a radiant rainbow. We are ecstatic. I hear that there is a pot of gold at the end of the rainbow. Honestly, I think that is a put-on story! I am quite proud to say I am worth more than my weight in gold, so I will not go digging for that pot. Jill and Mom race to the swing sets.

Mom wipes them dry, and they swing high, looking at the clouds, reaching the skies while the sounds of their laughter fill the air. Although she's an adult and a mother, Mom can still behave like a child when she abandons her cares. This is my *funnest* part. JF and PS frown and inform me that *funnest* is not a word; it should be *most fun.* Whatever! Anyhow, I have decided that I will *swing through life,* relishing each day.

Dancing in the rain (even though we were dancing indoors) is great fun, but be careful not to catch a cold. I am a little soggy, but I'm not complaining because I will dry out soon. We did have a lot of exercise today, and it was so enjoyable. I'm wishing you a fun day, too. Bye until our next adventure!

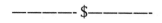

Activities

1. Like UDB, sit on the windowsill and watch the rain pouring outside. Do you notice the different shapes of the raindrops hitting the window and flowing down? Draw the various shapes you see.

2. Once you spot the rainbow, see if you can make out the colors. Figure out what ROY G. BIV stands for and match the colors.

3. You should not get *bored* on a rainy day, so bring out your *board* games to play with your friends and siblings.

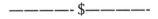

UDB Visits Grandma and Grandpa

big Cherry family get-together is planned for today at our grandparents' farm house. Feeling cramped, my friends, PS (not Pumpkin Seller, but Peter September), JF (not Joking Fun, but Jenni February), WO (not Warm Oats, but Wendy October), and I, UD (not Us Dogs, but Unique Dollar) Billy are ready for a new outing. Who knows what stains this new adventure will bring? You might remember, we are $1 bills with different unique markings reminding us of our past experiences. We have learned so much already, but still have a long ways to go. Pops January (PoJa) tells us to calm down in the wallet and be more patient and disciplined so we can grow up to be role models someday, but I don't want to grow up yet. I am having so much fun being one of the juniors in the wallet.

Visiting Grandma—fondly called Gma (pronounced Jeema) —and Grandpa—fondly called Gpa (pronounced Jeepa)—is always fun because they spoil the children and we get to taste so many goodies. Gma bakes endlessly, and Gpa shows us around the farm. There are so many animals and pets!

The station wagon is loaded, and Mom Cherry has cooked dishes to share that are in the cooler. The children are buckled in with their seatbelts, and we are off. Sandwiches and boxed drinks are passed around. After a few spills, the children fall asleep while we are driving on the highway. We must have entered country roads, as the noise has lessened. Dad and Mom Cherry take turns driving as we get to see rolling hills in the distance and picket fences surrounding acres of land. We are definitely in farming country now; we hear the grazing cows moo.

We drive up an endless driveway lined with beautiful trees, almost like a canopy welcoming us. Even before the car makes a full halt, the passenger doors open. The children fall into their grandparents' arms for huge hugs and kisses. A giggling Jill is lifted high up in the air by Gpa. The dogs, Milky, Paper, and Paws, are all over us, and we are soggy with their slobbering licks. Even the four cats have come out to see us. Everyone is so joyous, and there is much laughter as the children meet their cousins. There is so much deafeningly fun noise.

Gpa takes us to the cow barn. There is hay around us, and look there—an adorable calf. We surround and pet her until she gets tired and cuddles beside her mother. Gpa shows us how the milk is drawn from the cows through machines and collected into milk trucks that take them to pasteurizing units. Oh dear, another big word—what does it mean? Pasteuri ... why?! PS, who's been on a farm before, has a milk stain on his George Washington's mouth to prove it, so he explains that Pasteur is the name of a scientist who found that milk has bacteria that can cause it to spoil. Now, what is bacteria? It must be the area in the back that needs massaging so often. Have you noticed that questions seem to get answered with bigger words that need defining again? WO immediately points out that bacteria are the bad guys that could make you sick. Oh no, I don't want to be sick! When I get sick, I become all stiff and warm and sometimes have gooey stuff coming out of my George Washington's eyes and nose. Phew! Getting sick is terrible.

Meanwhile, PS wisely explains that high temperatures kill the bad guys, and once the milk is cooled after that, it can remain fresh in the refrigerator for a week or two. This preserves its nutritional qualities. Now I understand why everyone drinks so much milk. It is good for your body. I know it is good for the bones, but is it good for your brains, too? Do find out and let me know.

Who is ready for a snack at tea time? Gpa brings in some fresh milk for us to drink warm from the cow with cream floating on top. Now, why does cream float on top and not sit at the bottom? This time, JF answers that cream is just fat and is lighter than milk, so it floats. How can it be fat and light? Most fat people are heavy, right? I don't get it, but I'm eager to taste Gma's cookies. They are absolutely delicious, especially when they're dipped in the milk and the creamy hands find their way to us bills. My George Washington's mouth now has a brown stain from the chocolate chip cookies.

There are two horses at the farm, and we take carrots to them. Gpa does not allow the younger children to ride. However, Jim is allowed to sit on the pony while Gpa guides her around a small circle. The pony is so excited to see us that she pees all over the place. I see everyone holding their noses and moving away. Jim is caught on the horse, and he is laughing loudly. Gpa has a surprise treat for us. One by one, he takes the adults and the children for a ride on his tractor. Whoopee! The tractor makes a lot of noise and has a huge shovel in the front.

Gpa shows us how the land is tilled by picking up soil from one area and dumping it in another. Seated on Dad's lap, Brian asks for permission to operate the shovel. He hits the up button, and the shovel rises but does not stop, even as he hits the stop button multiple times. The tractor feels like a rearing horse as it moves with big jerky thuds. Oh, this is actually great fun. However, Brian is scared. Laughingly, dear Gpa shows him where the stop button is. Brian now hits the lowering button. This time, it hits the soil and digs right in. Gpa now takes charge and hits the correct buttons to move around the pit before we fall into it.

While the children are playing outside, the adults are busy fixing dinner. Brothers and sisters are having a great time laughing and exchanging stories about their lives. The men are tossing salads, and the women are removing many dishes from the oven—casseroles and other main entrees. Gma insists on baking her own breads using her secret recipes. Mmm, everything smells so delicious.

WO tells us to wait patiently until the family tastes them. Can't wait! I am already stretching, and my edges are peeking from the wallet. Grubby fingers find their way into pockets very shortly. WO and JF now have red tomato stains on their George Washingtons' arms. Here come the desserts, my favorite part. There are too many choices: warm pies with ice cream and cakes—yummy, yummy. No wonder the little ones are taught to say, "Yummy yummy for the tummy!"

The children get to spend the night in their parents' childhood rooms and sleep in bunk beds. Brian jumps up to the upper bed and makes himself comfortable. Jim, being the oldest, demands preference to choose first, and a fist fight ensues. Before the parents can mediate, Brian falls from the top. Immediately, Jim kindly picks him up to make sure he is not hurt. Meanwhile, naughty Jill climbs onto the upper bed by herself. The boys have lost the bed! The parents resolve the issue by telling them that since they would be spending three nights at Gma's, all three kids will get a turn to sleep on the upper bed. They are so tired after so much food and excitement that they fall asleep even before their parents can tuck them in.

The next morning, the children wake up early. Gpa has promised them a visit to the chicken barn. As they say, "Early to sleep and 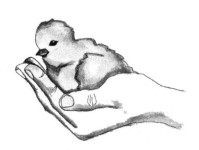 early to rise makes the children healthy, wealthy, and wise!" Jill runs into the barn and frightens the hens that go clucking around. She runs behind them, and they fly further away. Gpa manages to put a basket on one and hold it down for her. However, he tells her to be quiet so they can lay their eggs undisturbed. Jim is surprised, and he points to a basket with small chicks. They must have hatched just two days ago. They are so cute and little. Gpa lovingly holds them in his hand so the children can pet them. Dad collects the laid eggs and heads off to the kitchen.

Gma rings a bell, and children come running in for breakfast. In their enthusiasm, they fail to notice that Gma has placed a surprise boiled egg on each seat. Can you imagine if the children had sat on warm, just-boiled eggs? It would have scrambled the eggs and burnt their bottoms! Imagining this makes me rub my friends, and we burst into laughter in the wallet. I have always wondered if the chicken came first, or the egg. If you find the answer, please do let me know.

All good things must come to an end, and it is time to say our goodbyes. The car is loaded with gifts Gpa and Gma have showered on the children. They will have enough games to keep them occupied at least until we get home. They cry as they bid goodbye but are pacified by promises that Gma and Gpa will visit them soon. There is silence as the car leaves the farm, and we are on our way home. Partings are always sad, but we now look forward to our next adventure. Bye for now!

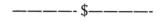

Activities

1. After your visit with your grandparents, write them a note about the fun things you liked doing with them.

2. At your next visit, help your grandparents with chores.

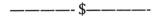

- 18 -

UDB Enjoys Halloween

Next week is Halloween. Have you noticed that it is usually the coldest and darkest day of fall? This year, my owners decide to go on outings and actually spook the children. My $1 friends, WO (not Winged Orangutan, but Wendy October) and JF (not Jolly Farmer, but Jenni February), two wimpy, scaredy-cat girls, are on either side of me, UDB (not Under Dog Buster, but Unique Dollar Billy). I don't know how I will keep them from screaming and hiding behind me. Although I am younger than they are, I will just have to be brave. My absent-minded owner Dad Cherry has forgotten his wallet and stashed us in his pocket. We actually like this, as we can see and hear better this way.

However, I miss PS (not Punky Style, but Peter September), who is at home, back in the wallet. We will have so much to tell him when we get back—that is, *if* we get back, with all the ghosts and skeletons roaming around.

Our first stop is at a pumpkin farm. The children run wild, trying to fill the cart little Jill rolls around. The boys are strictly told to choose only one pumpkin each. It must be a size that they alone must carry home. This is a hard decision. Brian chooses a huge pumpkin, but he can hardly lift it off the ground, so that one is out. Ooh! I spy an ideal weight orange pumpkin. Brian trips over a vine and lands face down next to it! He now sees and likes my find and manages to carry it to the car. Jim finds himself a larger yellow pumpkin that he can carry. Meanwhile, Jill loads her cart with several small ones. My favorite is an especially tiny speckled one. It's so cute!

A huge pick-up truck filled with hay gives rides to all. Jill sits on Dad's lap, but it is rather slippery. I hope Dad does not fall off the hay ride, as I am scared I will fall out of his pocket. Surprisingly, nothing happens, and all the passengers are okay. The children run from the hay ride to the corn maze. I like getting lost. As they say, there is always light at the end of the tunnel. There is no tunnel here, and it is easy to get lost! The corn has grown to heights above seven feet, and we try to follow previous footprints. With a wrong turn, we find ourselves in the middle, with many paths we can choose to follow. Dad smartly pulls out his compass, and we head north—hopefully towards the exit. Wrong again! The exit is towards the south (some helpful stragglers tell us). I hope this is not like the blind following the blind, if you know what I mean. In fact, the exit is toward the south, and we find ourselves in the open air very soon. Phew, that is a relief! Dad must have been quite worried for a while there. I see him wiping his sweaty brow.

Back at home, carving knives are on the table that is covered with newspapers. Butter-fingered Dad decides to show the children the trick to carving a pumpkin! I always knew that Dad was absent-minded, but I didn't know he dipped his fingers in butter all the time. Do you think he does this purposely to make carving easier? I guess I will have to wait and find out. He starts at the top, cuts and removes a lid, and scoops out the insides. Eeew, so many fibers and seeds! All this pulp mess slips through his butterfingers and spills all over the floor. Oh dear! Jill slips and falls into the cart that goes rolling around the kitchen. Dad rushes to stop the cart and slips and falls as well. The runaway cart hits a cabinet and stops. While Jill and Dad are helped off the floor, everyone is having a good laugh. Luckily, padded pants and shirts keep them unhurt, but we bills took a banging, alright.

Fortunately, we look around and find that none of us are torn or overly bent. Dad then cuts evil triangular eyes and decides to make a mouth with crooked teeth. However, the knife slips through his butterfingers (I am convinced they are buttered now) and slits a big, open mouth. Now the knife is stuck in the pumpkin. Actually, this has a rather scary effect, so they let the knife stick out (it's not that sharp, anyway)! Can you imagine a pumpkin with a knife sticking out from its mouth? By this time, the children are using their imaginations to carve their own pumpkins, with Mom Cherry helping to scoop out the pulp this time. The pumpkins are then placed on the front porch with electric candles inside. They will look spooky when they're lit in the evening.

Attending the Halloween class parties in school is so much fun, as the children are in costume and parade around the playground outdoors. There are way too many elves and goblins floating around. Healthy foods like whole wheat brownies with orange sprinkles, sweet potato chips, pumpkin pies, oranges, grapes, strawberries, and fruit juices are served. Jim is Superman, and Brian is a ninja warrior. Jill is allowed to attend both parties, and she is an angel with wings. Buying their costumes has been quite a challenge for Mom, as there are too many choices and too many ideas!

As Halloween evening descends, the porch is decorated with nylon spider webs. A scarecrow made of hay hangs from the fence. He has an orange top hat and a long carrot beak. There are orange electric spooky lights on the rose bushes that line the driveway. Orange and yellow chrysanthemum flower pots and the lighted carved pumpkins decorate the porch. Jill is tip-toeing around with her silver magic wand, touching things and hoping the pumpkin will turn into a carriage, like in Cinderella's fairy tale! The color scheme for Halloween is decidedly orange and yellow. Fall colors, of course!

Dad comes downstairs with a huge, red, bulbous nose. Oh dear! He must have fallen on his nose and bled. Not surprising, considering that he is a klutz. However, the children are excited to see their clown, who will escort them around the neighborhood. So, that is just a plastic nose—it must be the only thing he has to wear for a clown costume! Good thing he has not changed into the red boxer shorts he was threatening to wear. Come to think of it—the red shorts would have matched his red nose! Imagine the red nose and the red boxer shorts—ha!

Dad leaves us on the kitchen table, and I am told by both WO and JF that my costume looks good and suits me well. I am rather puzzled, as I did not change into any costume. However, they insist on telling me that I look like a pirate. A PIRATE? Can you believe that? It takes me a few moments to understand them. When I get it, I burst out laughing. I do agree with them. Me with my George Washington and his one black eye. Whoopee! I definitely look like a pirate and am totally dressed and ready for Halloween.

Meanwhile, costumed kids arrive at the door and ring the bell. Why do these kids say "Tick or Teeth" so fast? I have never seen "Ticking Teeth" before, have you? Who or what are these ticky teeth? Do they tick to the rhythm of drums beating in their heads? As the evening progresses, I understand they are saying "Trick or Treat." Mom hands out candy (the treats, I guess), but I still don't understand what "Trick" is. I think that she is tricking the children by hiding behind the door in a witch's costume and spooking them with a loud "Boo!" At least now I know who the "Trick-or-Treaters" are!

Every time Mom surprises the trick-or-treaters, I get scared and almost jump out of the wallet. My friends, WO and JF have to hold me in. I will never call them wimps again. They are more brave than me! We tell PS all about our outing, and he admits that he had so much space when we were gone, he stretched out and took a wonderful nap. He is not jealous but decides to make weird and scary "Boo" sounds along with Mom to frighten us (mostly me) in the wallet.

The children enter with their hoard of candy in little pumpkin baskets. I call it "loot." The parents must first examine them for contamination before they can be eaten. They have already had enough candy for one day and are very tired after so much excitement throughout the day. Hot chocolate with dinner does the trick, and they are ready for bed. I actually taste some candy from Dad's hands because he must have eaten some from Jill's loot. I do not taste any butter. How strange!

Just then, a young teenage girl arrives with a three-year-old girl in a snowflake costume and a four-year-old boy dressed as a huge orange pumpkin with a green hat. The pumpkin is an inflated balloon, and the boy is wobbly on his feet with so much air around his stomach. In any case, both look very cute. In his rush to get to the door, the little boy falls over the rose bushes. He escapes with a few scratches. However, the pumpkin costume has several holes from the rose bush thorns. Oh dear! It is deflated in minutes. The child is crying out loudly because his costume is totally ruined.

Mom comes to the rescue with a whole bunch of his favorite candy, which pacifies him immediately. While entering their driveway, Jill runs to the little boy and tells him not to cry, as she is willing to share her candy with him. They become instant friends and decide to meet for a playdate the next week. The teen introduces herself as the children's babysitter. Dad notices that she is doing a fine job taking care of the two children she is escorting around. He asks her for her name and telephone number for future use and, incidentally, he gifts two of us bills to her. I find myself in her backpack now.

Goodnight and congratulations on a good candy haul this year.

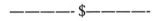

Activities

1. Way before next Halloween, discuss your costumes with your parents. Draw them pictures of the characters and costumes.

2. Help your parents decorate the house to make it spooky.

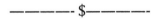

UDB Travels with the Babysitter

The parents of Daniel III (ten years old), and Danielle (five years old) have a babysitter care for their two children while they attend a dinner party. Now, why would you give your children such names? Daniel is called "Dan" by his friends and "Junior" by his parents. You might have rightly guessed that his dad and grandfather are both Daniels, too. Danielle is fondly called Dally. Watch out—she might be teased in school for dilly-dal-lying! I hope she does not live up to her name. This family makes me wonder if there is a shortage of names on Earth.

Mom Brown decides to pay the babysitter, Kimmy, who lives down the street, as soon as she shows up. This way, she will not need to look for change at the last minute at night. Guess what? Some of my friends are handed over to fourteen-year-old Kimmy, who stuffs them in a pouch in her open backpack with me. I look around and find myself among a few $20 and $10 elders and those nosy $5 bills. I am beside myself with joy, and my edges wave wildly as I spot my good buddy, $1 AB (Auggie, August Bill). You might remember he is one of the "Three Billeteers" and unique with his bespectacled George Washington. He spies me, too, and with each movement of the backpack, we inch closer until we can hug one another. It has been a long time since I saw him. We have so much to talk about.

We also befriend another $1 bill. His name is Dustin March. He has brown specks all across his note and is fondly called Dust Mite.

Before leaving, the Mom confides in Dad Brown that she is *distressed*. Kimmy may be too young to take care of naughty Dally. Did I hear *destressed?* Why would she be *destressed* and still look so troubled? Words have such different meanings—or maybe they sound alike but have different spellings with different meanings? I am puzzled. However, here comes Auggie to the rescue. He tells me that words like distressed and destressed are called *homophones*—like home phones? I wonder if Auggie has become more academic, or denser!

After his parents leave, Junior is highly grumpy. He cannot find his homework sheets, and until he finishes his homework, he is not allowed to watch his favorite TV show. Dally has this habit of hiding Junior's homework so she can get more time to play with him, and she refuses to reveal her secret hiding place. Kimmy is thinking of ways to get her to give it back to her brother. Kimmy removes her sneakers at the bottom of the stairs and joins Dally on the carpet so they can play dress-up with her dolls. Then they play "sharing secrets," and Dally reveals that Junior's homework is under her bed.

They both run to Dally's bedroom. Crawling under the bed, she hands the homework to Kimmy. While crawling out,  her toe gets stuck at one end of the sheets, and soon the comforter and sheets fall over both girls. Junior hears laughter, and when he arrives, he finds both the girls under a pile of sheets as if they are in a tent. He pulls his giggling sister out, and then both kids help Kimmy redo Dally's bed.

While Kimmy and Dally were looking for his homework, Junior was pouting. Oh dear! This means he was up to some quiet mischief. He found Kimmy's sneakers in the hallway, and guess what he did? He tied together the laces of the two shoes and left them in the hallway.

Although Dally is the talkative one, Junior is the real naughty one.

Dally now spends time rifling through Junior and Kimmy's backpacks. Through her grubby fingers, we get to taste chocolate chip cookies. Oh, so chewy! Meanwhile, Junior is struggling with his spelling words and whines that they are too hard. Dally suggests they play school, as she is fascinated by the books in the backpacks. Kimmy thinks that is a good idea and becomes the teacher. She reads out the words slowly and *phonetically* (what is that—a tickly phone?) to help Junior spell. First, we have *home phones,* and now *tickly phones.* What's with phones and homework today?

Feeling left out, Dally throws a tantrum and yells, "I hate you!" at Junior. Kimmy says that's *demeaning.* What is the meaning of *hate?* In a teacher-like manner, she explains that first, hate is too harsh a word; second, one should not hate anyone; and third, it is not dignified to use such words. Even I get the meaning of *demeaning* and *hate* now. Sheepishly, Dally hugs her brother and tells him how much she loves him. She likes her brother a lot, so she actually does not hate him. It is a disrespectful word. All this does not stop Junior from worrying about his spelling words.

Kimmy, who is a whiz at math, asks him to finish his math homework first. Taking a break always helps to let the mind breathe a bit, I suppose. Junior's math homework does not take long at all, so Junior must be a math whiz, too. Then they get back to tackling the spelling words again. Since Junior is familiar with the sounds, he is now able to spell almost all of them correctly. So, *phonetically* must mean sounding the words. This time, it is I who tell Auggie and Dust Mite that there is no *tickling phone.* If a word is phonetically correct, it makes spelling it easier. At least I got this one before smartie Auggie. *Nanny-nanny-boo-boo*, as Dally would say.

Junior is having trouble with *quite* and *quiet.* He asks Kimmy to put both words into sentences. She puts a finger across her lips. Dally immediately says hush, be *quiet.* Junior gets it instantly. Dally is one smart cookie. She may start spelling all of Junior's words before getting to fourth grade. Junior spells *quite* correctly too as Kimmy says, it is *quite* simple. Phew! The homework is all done and stowed away in the backpack.

Junior and Dally watch TV for a bit while Kimmy scoops out ice cream for all of them. They deserve this treat after doing their homework so quickly. Dust Mite is a great fan of butterscotch, and he jumps above us, hoping Kimmy will search her backpack for something. He doesn't have to wait long. She digs into her backpack to take out her homework, hoping to finish it while the children are asleep. They love their sitter, and Kimmy knows she can always call her parents if needed. The two children are soon in their pajamas but insist on Kimmy reading to them while they are in bed. Kimmy is very willing to oblige. She reads aloud a story for her book report that's due tomorrow. She tries to kill two birds with one stone. Dust Mite gets it first this time. I get it too, although I would not want to hurt the birds, much less kill them.

While Dally is fast asleep, Junior closes his eyes but does not sleep yet. He is actually waiting for his parents to get home. Soon after they arrive, he hears the big thud that he has been waiting for. He runs out of his room and snoops from the landing. Laughing to himself, he jumps into bed, pretending to be fast asleep. What do you think happened? Kimmy puts on her sneakers while busily talking with his parents. As usual, she does not tie her laces. One step and she lands on the floor, spilling the contents of her backpack everywhere. Although she's physically unhurt, she is embarrassed. The parents get her off the floor and smilingly admit that only their mischievous son, Junior, would have thought this one up.

Laughing at being tricked, she ties her shoes properly this time. She realizes that she must get over this bad habit of not lacing her shoes promptly. She has tripped on her laces before, even without the two shoes tied together! Funny, but dangerous. Also, she should leave shoes in the closet and not in plain view where children can play with them. All in all, lessons are learned.

Finding the children asleep, Dad Brown is so pleased that he offers to drop Kimmy home and hands her an *envelope*. Did I hear *and we elope?*

How can he elope, or run away with her? I don't get it. Maybe there is something in the packet that will help Kimmy elope with a boyfriend, whom I know nothing about. I don't even know if a boyfriend exists. I think she is rather young to elope. Now I am *distressed* not *destressed.* Finally, I get it! I am indeed *distressed!* Kimmy finds extra money in the packet, so *envelope* must mean the packet and have nothing to do with eloping. Gosh, I am so relieved.

I inch closer to Auggie and Dust Mite to hear about their adventures. There is so much space and noise in Kimmy's backpack that we can stretch and crackle aloud. No one will disturb us or yell at us for being loud; the elders are busily gossiping, too. As much as I like Kimmy, I am relieved I don't need a babysitter. I must admit, sometimes these elders can be rather bossy. We $1 bills now have time to catch up with friends, old and new buddies. You should try it too. I am sure you will love it and have as much fun as we are having. If you have finished your homework and are in bed, we bills wish you a goodnight! Sweet dreams!

—————- $ —————-

Activities

1. Try to cooperate with your baby sitter. Take out books that you would like her/him to read to you.

2. Write down your spelling words and ask the babysitter to quiz you. Also, ask for help with the meanings of the hard words.

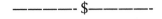

—————- $—————-

- 20 -

UDB is Dog Walking and Cat Sitting

Kimmy, my present owner, is an ambitious fourteen-year-old and a good babysitter. She loves cats and dogs, so she assumes she can offer cat and dog sitting and walking services, too. If only she would take the time to sort out her backpack. I guess I should not complain, as I have a lot of space to spread myself right now. At least I am not crammed into a wallet or purse. Plus, I have my $1 buddies, August Bill (Auggie) and Dustin March (Dust

Mite). You might remember that Auggie's George Washington has eyeglasses drawn over the eyes.

I was told that Kimmy is a good *doodler.* That must be why she calls everyone a cool *dude!* Dust Mite complains that while Kimmy was doodling, she looked at Auggie's glasses and drew one heart-shaped eye on his George Washington—only on one eye! He whines, wishing she could have drawn some cool-looking glasses and not a heart-shaped eye. Now I see it and understand that *doodling* must mean scribbling or drawing wildly. I tease him because it makes him a little girlish looking, heart and all. However, I do think he looks cool. They both like my George with his one blackened eye as it makes me easily recognizable. In any case, I am proud of it and my other marks.

Being good at doodling, Kimmy makes these squiggly lettered flyers in neon colors and posts them on the lamp posts near her house. Her parents have forbidden her to bring home any cats and dogs but have allowed her to do pet walking and sitting in their neighborhood. First, she must convince them that her homework is finished. This will teach Kimmy to manage her time better, I think. These teenagers are all over the place otherwise. In fact, I am envious of them sometimes. They tell each other so many interesting stories using words such as, *like, um, dude, man whatever, totally, etc.* I must admit, I am not good at teen language, "slang" as they call it, so I don't always get it. Anyway, it doesn't matter so much nowadays as they text each other all the time. Even from the bathroom! During class they are supposed to switch off their phones, but I am not so sure. We hear a lot of texts going back and forth there, too: a constant click, click, click.

We get bumped around a lot in Kimmy's backpack, and we have scratches and wrinkles to prove it. We are not starched anymore, so we stretch out and reach each other quite easily. It feels good to relax. Today, when Kimmy reaches home, she receives a call from the old lady next door, who needs help with her dog and cat. It is wintertime, and she does not want to go walking outside and catch a cold. Kimmy is delighted to help; the old lady always gives her generous tips for helping her with errands.

Kimmy finishes her homework quickly and rushes off to her neighbor's. There is only a covering of snow in the driveway, so she decides that should be no problem. She feeds Milky, the cat; gives her milk, which she loves; and changes the litter box. While she is petting Milky, the dog, Pilo, is anxious to go out and pulls her jeans. She gets her coat, gloves, hat, and backpack (she never goes anywhere without us and her phone in it), puts a leash on Pilo, and off they go for their walk/run. *Brr!* It's freezing outside.

Kimmy's backpack is always half open—these teens! I peek to see smoke coming out of Kimmy's mouth. I am astonished, as I did not know that she smokes. It is so bad for her health. I feel a whack from one of Auggie's edges. He tells me that it is only air *condensing.* Something is singing, but what or who is *conden?* An exasperated Auggie explains that the air from her mouth is warm, and when it hits the cold outside, it *condenses.* I still don't get it, *dense* as I am. He patiently tells me that *condensing* means becoming moist so it looks like smoke. I am so relieved that she is not smoking. Pilo's breath is also condensing, and even I know that dogs don't smoke.

Kimmy has brought a plastic bag to scoop the poop. She holds her breath (no vapor) and scoops it quite efficiently. Every so often, though, Pilo goes off to sniff the trees and grass and so on. Kimmy gives him a long leash, but when she sees other walkers or runners, she reigns him in. I do think that she is a very good pet walker and sitter. She returns and takes a huge tip home. Quite happy with herself, she feels that she is now ready to walk more dogs. However, this time she decides to take them all out at the same time. Remember, I told you she was ambitious. Let's see how she fares with three dogs.

Fortunately, the dogs are good friends because they're neighbors. Kimmy picks them up from three different homes, so now we have Pilo (a German Shepherd), Simo (a Dachshund), and Cookie (a Great Dane). Can you imagine walking three dogs of different sizes on three leashes? Good luck, is what I say. Pilo is the friendliest of them and is a good-sized dog, Simo is a short dog with an elongated back, and Cookie is a thin dog, but very tall.

Kimmy is brave and waits patiently to pick up their poops. However, each goes sniffing in different directions. She has to keep calling out their names to make them go at a slower pace to accommodate Simo. Dust Mite tells me that even though they are good friends, the dogs' *gaits* are different. I don't see any gates around. We are on a sidewalk with no fences. Dust Mite tells us to notice how each of the dogs walk. They are different, with small and big paces. I immediately get it—*gaits* must mean styles of walking.

Suddenly, a squirrel scuttles across our path. The dogs go wild. They bark, straining at their leashes while Kimmy tries to hold on tight to all three of them. One leash gets loose, and Cookie takes off. Meanwhile, the other two run around and around Kimmy. Her feet get caught in the leashes, and she falls with a big thud. She looks like a *mummy,* all wrapped up. This reminds me of a wad of $20 bills wrapped in paper with a rubber band around them. It is funny, and I do feel like laughing, but I hope Kimmy is not hurt.

The two dogs are forced to stop, although they pull her a few yards onto the grass. This is a good thing. A pedestrian rushes across to help Kimmy unwind herself and help her up. She is laughing along with the kind gentleman from up the street, so she must be alright. She looks around and realizes that Cookie is missing. She hands the two leashes to the gentleman and asks him to wait until she finds Cookie. Being a Great Dane whose gait is pretty large, Cookie may have gone far by now. Calling her name, Kimmy frantically runs down the road.

By this time, Cookie has stopped to pee and is near a tree at the end of the road. Kimmy rushes to catch her leash, then pets and cuddles her. What would she have said to the owners if Cookie had run away and she could not be found? She learned a lesson today that it is better to walk one dog at a time. Many dogs might have worked if the dogs were almost the same size, but I still have my doubts.

Meanwhile, the kind gentleman offers to walk Pilo and Simo home. However, Kimmy realizes that it is her responsibility, so she returns them to their owners while thanking the gentleman profusely. She rushes to get Cookie home. By this time, it has become bitterly cold, and the driveway is covered with sleet and ice. Kimmy holds on to the leash tightly. However, Cookie's paws slide, and whoa! We all find ourselves sliding down the driveway at great speed like we're in a toboggan race. We soon land with Cookie on top of us. That was actually a lot of fun while it lasted. The air is very cold, so I am grateful that we stopped.

Kimmy continues to help her neighbors during winter. This winter has been particularly severe, with a lot of snowfall. The white lawns and roofs of houses covered in many inches of snow look beautiful. It's almost like Winter Wonderland. Soon the weather warms up a bit, and it starts raining. Kimmy first feeds Milky and lets her out, and then walks Pilo.

Suddenly, as they come up the driveway, all the piled-up snow on the roof comes sliding down. Kimmy finds herself with Pilo, Milky, and a lot of wet snow on top of her. She gets up totally drenched and realizes that while Milky was on the roof, she must have dislodged the snow and caused this *avalanche*. I don't know yet what *avalanche* means, but it is no wonder they say, "It's raining cats and dogs!" *Avalanche* must mean a lot of snow or rain, as it is pouring now.

Soon the grass will be green and the white snow will be gone. I can't wait for spring. However, I must admit it has been lovely accompanying Kimmy on her dog walks and cat-sitting adventures. I hope you are also a dog and cat lover. Just like her, you can offer to help your neighbors with their dogs and cats too. Then, you will get to pet and cuddle with them as well. Kimmy is considering giving up her babysitting services and becoming a pet sitter instead. Either way, she will learn to become more responsible and manage her time better. Do whatever you can to help your neighbors. Happy sitting and walking!

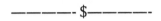

Questions/Activities

1. Do you like dogs? Help your dog walker to walk one small dog. Did you check if the dog tags are on the collar?

2. Do you like cats? Help your neighbor to feed the cat.

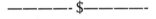

- 21 -

UDB is Stuck in a Traffic Jam

O ut of the blue, we hear Kimmy's cell phone ringing. It turns out to be Mr. Brown, who asks her to stop by to arrange schedules and settle payments for the babysitting job she did earlier. While Kimmy is giving back change, I find that I am transported from Kimmy's backpack to Mr. Brown's wallet.

The next day, Mr. Brown drives up to celebrate the holiday weekend with his family. In fact, I, UDB (Unique Dollar Billy) am stuck between Delia December (DeeDee) and May June (MJ—she could not decide whether she was born in May or in June!) Have you ever been scrunched between two girls before? Especially $1 girl bills? Let me tell you, it isn't easy. Dee Dee has streaming lines (like streamers) radiating from a circular "D" next to her George Washington. Maybe that is why she is named DeeDee (repeated Ds) since her "D" is emphasized so it's twice as bold. MJ has a long necklace drawn around her George Washington's collar, and boy, does she know how to swing that around as she tries to "unscrunch" or stretch herself. Although he's a bit girly, her George looks almost majestic in some ways, with a pearl necklace and all—he's almost like a king from Asia. Speaking of kings, I wave to my old $1 buddie, July King (JK) in the wallet. He looks like a British King with a crown drawn on his George Washington's head.

George Washington was appointed Commander-in-Chief of the Continental Army in 1775, during the

American Revolution. He was against tyranny. I know this word has nothing to do with rainy Ts, so I nudge JK to tell me what it means. Patiently, he explains that tyranny means the cruel and unfair treatment of people. Washington never used his powers unwisely, and he later became the first President of the United States. Can you imagine that? It is his face that is printed on us $1 bills! I am convinced that we must be just as important as he was. Washington certainly would not want a crown on his head. However, since it is drawn on JK's George, I will tease him by bowing down to him.

Alright now, that's enough for a history lesson. Back to battling traffic. We've made good time so far, driving at a good pace for many hours. However, in the last few hours, with heavy traffic, we have been just crawling. Mrs. Brown says she will never travel in a car on a holiday weekend again. The two children, Dan (age ten) and Danielle (Dally for short, age five), are whining, "When will we get there?" again and again. They have been squabbling this entire time, with Dally sitting in her booster seat at the back. Mr. Brown is unable to understand why traffic is so *appalling.* Oh my, what a big word! I wonder what it means? It must be something to do with an *app calling* an iPhone. These days, apps on everybody's phones seem to be *in.* Hopefully, when the app calls, the traffic will magically disappear!

Suddenly, a sign appears that says there's a toll ahead. Mr. Brown says he has an EZ Pass, but he is not sure if it has enough money loaded on it. That must mean they can only go through the booth if they pass some test easily. No wonder there are innumerable rows of cars going through the booth ever so slowly. I hope we don't get asked a trick question after sitting in the car so long and barely moving a few miles. Mr. Brown takes out his wallet and pulls out the $1 bills— DeeDee, MJ, JK, and me—and places us on the dashboard. Freedom at last! We decide to make the most of it and slowly stretch and peek around.

All we can see is a sea of cars in front of us until the back of beyond—or should I say *front of beyond?* Mr. Brown manages to get into a lane that says *EZ Pass and Exact Cash* (which must mean us four $1 bills.) This must mean every car must pass a test with an easy question to get through the toll. Although I am excited to hear the question, I am scared that if we don't pass the test, we will be handed over to the cashier as hostage for the car to proceed. JK knocks me with one of his sharp edges and asks me to be patient and see what happens. Car after car passes, and when we get to the booth, there is no human there.

A green sign flashes saying *paid,* and we zoom through, though we don't go very far. Mr. Brown is quite proud of himself. He comments that he is glad he had set up his EZ Pass to auto reload. This must mean that the sticker on his windshield is the EZ Pass that has enough money for the tolls. Whew! That's a relief. For all my worrying, there were no questions and no pop quizzes. In a way, I am glad, because I was not traded away.

As we get through the booth, we are really in a jam. It is starting to become dark, and cars are putting on their lights. Six lanes have now merged into two to enter the next expressway. Oh my. We see nothing but here a car, there a car, everywhere a car, car! We are happy to be forgotten on the dashboard, and we are able to see red lights all around us. I am fascinated by the red brake lights going on and off in the bumpers ahead of us. More on than off, mind you. Have you ever paid attention to the shapes of the tail lights? My friends and I play a game by calling out the shapes of the lights.

A cute car with winking eyes is trying to edge in front us. It looks like round pupils on each side are sliding on lower eyelids. Her lights go on and off. It's almost a squint now, with both pupils trying to roll inwards. Gosh, she hasn't stopped winking at me since I set eyes on her. She seems to be a regular winker. I call my cutie "Winky." She does get her way; we are forced to let her merge in with her winking left turn lights! MJ spots a big van with huge cat's eyes. The van looks like a mean leopard trying to block out other cars. She names her car "Wildcat." Funnily enough, it has a placard at the back that reads, "Beware of Dogs." I think it should be "Beware of Cats!"

Meanwhile, DeeDee almost jumps off the dashboard. She spots a car with an upturned moustache. This one actually looks scary. She calls her car "Macho."

JK smugly spies a big SUV with slanted eyes lifted at both ends. "Looks like a *samurai,"* he says while lifting all four corners of his bill. I don't know who or what a *samurai* is—there is no Sam in the car. Flapping his edges, he laughs and tells us that samurais are ancient Japanese warriors. Just then, the SUV honks and aggressively merges in front of us. It sure seems like a "warrior" car. We then see many cars with lights in the shapes of several round pupils, vertical lines, horizontal lines, triangles, and even some with lines going all the way across from one end to the other. An illuminated Jeep comes close to us. It looks cool with jazzy disco lights all around.

I never realized how many kinds of cars and how many kinds of tail lights are manufactured these days. Gosh, you will not believe what I just saw! Tail lights with small wipers! Actually, a miniature version of windshield wipers. I am sure these are useful during fog and rain/snow storms. The opposite side now has a stream of blue, white, and yellow lights, and our side has a sea of red lights. They look like beautiful, gem-studded, sparkling jewelry, as long as they are moving and not stuck. There are so many fun things to observe and learn.

Mrs. Brown says we are now approaching a *gigantic* bridge. *Jigantic?* It must mean the bridge sways so it is up to some jig, an Irish dance, and antics, or mischief. In any case, it is lighted on both sides and looks beautiful. The children are excited, and Mrs. Brown again points out how huge and gigantic it is. Oh, so *gigantic* means huge. No swaying or swinging, I suppose. We actually see a lighted ship in the distance—or should I say a gigantic ship? Meanwhile, we are still going bumper to bumper and after what seems to be an hour, we are finally off the bridge.

Suddenly, we hear sirens behind us. Several cop cars try to rush past us. Cars are moving left and right to make room for them. Brake lights are turning on and off. The dashboard reveals glints of light shining off several coins and keys way towards the windshield. We had not noticed them earlier, as the coins were separated and not noisily clinking today. No rest for us; Mr. Brown suddenly hits the brake hard, and the coins and some other things fly past us. DeeDee lands on top of me, but fortunately some keys land on top of us, keeping us safe on the dashboard. A pair of dark glasses lands on Mrs. Brown's lap. She is most surprised to find her long-lost pair! The coins land on the floor and will need to be collected after the Browns get to their destination.

We are back to moving at a snail's pace. MJ says this time traffic is slow due to *rubbernecking.* She must know what that means, as I don't. Flaunting her necklace, she explains that wherever there is an accident, people slow down and strain to look—they are rubbernecking. I get it! I now rubberneck to see what is happening. Fortunately, it is only a *fender bender,* I am told. Must mean a bumper bang leading to a bender! At such a slow pace, no one is hurt. To get through twenty miles, it has taken almost two hours on an expressway! At this rate, they may need to redefine expressway. Maybe it should be called a "snail's-pace-way!"

I have been wondering why no app has called yet, as we are still stuck in traffic. Mr. Brown is getting tired, and he again remarks that traffic today is awful and appalling. Oh dear! I now realize that *appalling* refers to the awful or terrible traffic, and not an app. Poor Mr. Brown. As we take our final exit, traffic clears, and we are ten minutes away from our destination. While I have enjoyed being on the dashboard all this time, I am getting cold, and I want to get back to my comfortable wallet surroundings. I cannot imagine that I am actually saying this! Actually, it is DeeDee who is the coldest, as she's on the top. The car halts, and Mr. Brown grabs us and puts us away in his wallet. As he has been sitting for so long on his wallet in the pocket of his jeans, we feel warm and safe already.

We hear many excited voices as the children delightedly meet their cousins. This is the real fun part. Driving does have its rewards, but being stuck in traffic does become tedious. Mrs. Brown again says there will be no more driving on a holiday weekend. That must mean that next time, they will fly or take the train. Well, that's something to look forward to. We shall see; driving is the cheapest way to see family. Even without doing the actual driving, my friends and I are rather tired. Siesta time!

The next day, we are forced to drive to the grocery store and have to stop by a tollbooth. Oh, dear! I am handed to the lady in the booth. Unfortunately, one needs exact change in coins to let the car through. Almost instantaneously, we hear a lot of honking from behind us. I hear JK remark that a human second is the

time between a light turning green (as in "paid" at the booth) and the first honk from the vehicle behind.

How impatient can you get? And that's after being in crawling traffic until now!

The kind lady quickly puts me away in the cash register and takes out—or shall I say, gets rid of—coins to make change. She drops the change in the basket to let us drive through. Patiently, she wishes everybody a safe and wonderful happy holiday. I, too, wish each and everyone of you a happy holiday with family and friends!

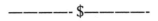

Questions/Activities

1. Can you identify the make of the car by the brake lights? Play a game the next time you are caught in a traffic jam. See who can name at least five cars first.

2. Sing songs and ask each other riddles when you are in a jam. Try not to disturb the driver.

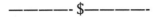

- 22 -

UDB Plays in the Snow

Since it's winter, it is cold outside, as it should be. Mom Deere goes to the bank, and I find myself in her handbag. Mom's two children, Sid (ten years old) and Teresa (Terry, twelve years old), are finishing their homework this evening. Their Dad just returned home, complaining that it was snowing intermittently outside, and traffic was consequently a mess. Gosh, he is speaking in riddles. What is intermitten? He must need mittens instead of driving gloves, which are probably not warm enough in this weather, and consequeen—I can't imagine how a queen can also be a con artist, if you know what I mean. Oh, dear, I am so ignorant. I will need to ask one of my smart buddies what these hard words mean later. Meanwhile, I find myself among nine other $1 bills. We look like a clone of cards, like a fan in the hands of a card player. Did you know that the number 9 is rather unique, like you and me? Every multiple of 9 adds up to a 9. For example: 9X2 = 18. 1+8 adds up to a 9. Isn't that strange and interesting? Try it out yourself and see.

Terry asks Mom for lunch money, as it is "dress day." Terry attends a private school where all students must wear a uniform every day. So "dress days" are special, and students look forward to them eagerly. This time, to dress down it is four dollars, and to dress up, it is three. Who wants to dress up to go to school? Mom hands me and two of my buddies to her. I am now in Terry's pencil box with Merry May (M&M 1), Munch March (M&M 2)—fancy that—and Jack January (JJ).

JJ's nickname, Jumping Jack, suits him to a T. This guy cannot keep still for a single minute. One dirty glare from MoMa Mother March, our $20 mentor, is all he needs to settle down, though. This young fellow's edges are crushed, and his George Washington looks rather crumpled. His jumpiness must have caused all the wrinkles! I am sure you remember me, Unique Dollar Billy (UDB), with my George and his one blackened eye.

We bills find ourselves crushed between blunt pencils and caps of ballpoint pens. That is not so bad. However, what hurts are the sharp pencils and the open ballpoint pens with their extended writing sharp points. I am especially wary of one red pencil with a pointy edge. She has already made a red slash on my back side. My White House looks all cross now. Although some part of it is Jack's jittery nature, Ms. Red Pencil has colored his George's face. Now he has a red, wrinkled George! Somehow, we manage to sleep through the night.

The next morning, Terry stuffs us four $1 bills in her back pocket before opening her curtains. Wow, there is a blanket of snow outside! Almost a foot has fallen overnight. It looks like Winter Wonderland and is beautiful! Everything is covered with white snow, and guess what? It continues to fall. Both Terry and Sid come racing downstairs with their backpacks to the aroma of waffles. Mom tells them that schools are closed today. You cannot imagine how loudly they screamed, "Whoopie! Snow day!" As Terry touches her pocket, we taste the yummy waffles and maple syrup. The only problem is that we then stick to each other until we dry out. Despite this discomfort, Mom's delicious cooking makes the stickiness worthwhile.

Dad is outside shoveling the driveway. He is still hoping to drive to work. He comes in with mittens but is bitterly complaining about the intermittent snowfall that has dumped more than a foot in their driveway. Seeing my puzzled expression, M&M1 explains that the snow did not come down continuously yesterday. Snowfall was intermittent. I get it! It is not about the mittens, then. The snow was dumped in stops and starts. I can now see how this could cause traffic jams. Oh, so consequently is not about a con queen. It means *therefore.* How foolish can I be? Mom invites Dad to the table for warm waffles and gives him the good news that all government offices are closed. The TV news channel is listing all the closings as the weatherperson predicts more snow! We see pictures of the salt trucks on major highways, but Dad remarks that our road might have to wait a day or two to be dug out.

Meanwhile, Sid and Terry wear their snow pants, warm hooded jackets, heavy gloves, caps, and ear muffs as they get ready to go out in the snow. The doorbell rings, and their friends Matt and Sara are waiting outside with their sleds. Did I say sleds? They look more like huge saucers. My friends and I are so excited to go sledding! JJ cannot be contained. MoMa is not with us to calm him down. One after the other, both M&Ms give him a firm bashing on his George's head to stop his crazy jumping around. We are in Terry's pocket, rearing to go. The cold hits, and we become a little stiff. However, the pocket is pretty warm, so we are in for a good time.

The kids walk up a small hill that, to us bills, feels like a huge mountain with a great slope. There are already many children sledding. The sounds of laughter are such a joy. Sid climbs behind Matt, as does Terry behind Sara. At the count of three, both saucers get a push from the passengers, and off they go down the hill! Oh, this is so much fun. JJ says it's so exhilarating. What's that? Rating this hill? JJ snickers and asks how I am feeling right now. I don't know why he needs to know, as all of us are feeling great. "That's exactly it," he remarks. So *exhilarating* means feeling great, like refreshing when the breeze blows snow at you as you slide downwards. Now the children have to lug the saucers and themselves uphill. This feels like climbing the Himalayas, a large mountain range in India, Nepal, and China!

On the third run, the boys and girls decide to race. This time the passenger at the back pushes the driver, and at the last minute jumps aboard behind the driver. The race has begun, and we are going really fast now. Wow! What an exhilarating feeling! Suddenly, Sid's boot gets caught on a branch, and Matt is bumped high. He goes flying over Sid. Meanwhile, the girls directly behind hit Matt, and they, too, go sprawling on the snow. Sara is performing strange somersaults, unable to stop, and the other three are in a pile on top of each other like a football pileup! Meanwhile, the saucers are sliding down the hill, one behind the other. It looks like they are having a lot of fun. Finally, they come to a halt at road level, which is almost two hills down. Uncomplainingly, the kids pick themselves up and trudge down to retrieve their "sleds." They are cold, and their noses and cheeks are red! It reminds me of Rudolph, the red-nosed reindeer! They head home to hot chocolate and warm chocolate chip cookies.

Mom tells them to take off their wet boots, hats, and gloves on a plastic sheet she spreads out near the door. The girls are busily jabbering away for a while and then decide to go out again to make snow angels in the front yard. Children never seem to mind the cold. Guess what? The boys come running out, too. Soon all four of them are on their backs, swishing their arms and legs. When they get u,p they see their artwork: beautiful angels with wings. Sara, the naughty one, makes a small ball of snow and hurls it at Matt. This starts a snowball fight. This time, it is each of them on their own—no teams. They run around the yard throwing snowballs, big and small, and wet snow on each other. Soon they collapse on the snow, exhausted.

Terry suggests they stop fighting and make a snowman. The boys roll a big ball and station it right in front of their living room bay window. The girls roll over a smaller ball. It requires all four of them to lift and put it on top of the lower big ball. Sara runs in to get a carrot for his nose and two coals from the fireplace for eyes. Matt attaches two branches for arms while Sid removes his cap and places it rather crookedly on the head. They move back to see a handsome, stout snowman. It's almost a landmark to their house.

It's time for Sara and Matt to go home for lunch. Sid somehow looks different. I see it now—he has gray hair. Snow is melting on his head—that's what happens without a hat. After lunch, Dad has a big surprise for the family. He bought walking skis for all four of them. The children are so excited. They beg to go to the park immediately. As the snow truck has not shoveled their street, they walk over to the adjacent golf course. With their ski boots and poles, they look like pros. Dad makes the tracks, with Sid and Terry following. Mom brings up the rear. The scenery is stunning. Trees have snow hanging from their branches. You can see white all around you. Over to the left, there is a little pond. The sides are frozen, and we see two ducks coming our way. Terry tries to run toward them. Oh dear, she falls because she forgets she has skis on. Mom hands her some bread for the hungry ducks. The sun is setting, and the snow reflects the red and orange hues.

We go back home to hot soup and pizza. Everyone is tired, but who doesn't want dessert? Dad has a roaring fire going in the fireplace. Mom brings out long skewers for making "s'mores," short for "some mores."

Have you had them before? Like the name implies, you cannot stop eating them. In between layers of cookies, there are slivers of chocolate and marshmallow. As the chocolate and marshmallow melt, they pull their skewers out, eat the some mores, and cannot stop licking their fingers.

Since it is a snow day, Sid and Terry can watch TV for a while before getting ready for bed. Gosh, it has been such an action-packed day. We bills are totally exhausted and ready to wind down. I hope Terry decides to get to bed soon. Yes, she is tired and sleepy, too. Goodnight until another snow day! Who knows? At this rate with more snow falling, it might be as soon as tomorrow!

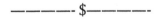

Questions/Activities

1. What games do you like to play with your friends in the snow? Draw a picture of you and your friends in the snow.

2. When entering the house, please put away wet gear on mats near the door. Help your parents to make hot chocolate to warm you up after being out in the cold.

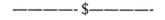

UDB Goes to CAMP DESTINY

Summer is approaching, and Mom and Dad Deere are looking into camps for siblings Sid (ten years old) and Teresa (Terry, twelve years old.) The children are ready to attend camp as long as their friends Matt (nine) and Sara (eleven) join them. Since all four want to be in the same camp, this now involves four adults agreeing on one camp. To make a decision, they decide to meet with a camp counselor who recommends an ideal camp. The brochure looks great, with fancy pictures of laughing children. The camp is in the mountains and offers activities like hiking, boating, camp fires, and more. It does seem ideal for the nine-to-twelve-year-olds, and it should excite all the four hard-to-please children with different interests. Believe me, making all four happy is not an easy task.

I am rather cramped in Dad's wallet and find myself between one-dollar bills Selfie September (SS—sounds more like the Secret Service) and Molly July (MJ—sounds more like Molly Jolly.) These two are actually great fun to be with. They constantly argue, and I am caught in between their bickering. SS is a kind of bleached green color from all the flash photography. After all, he is not named Selfie for nothing! He, unfortunately, sometimes tends to boast. However, MJ is good fun. She tells me she has a ready repartee for everything Selfie says. I guess repartee must mean going to a party again. Maybe she will explain it to me later.

SS has ear phones drawn around his George Washington's ears. He could actually belong to the Secret Service! MJ has huge ring earrings drawn around her George's ears. Whenever she moves, the earrings sway quite delightfully. Last but not least, I hope you remember me. I am Yours Truly, UDB, Unique Dollar Billy, with one blackened eye on my George.

Registration is completed, and a whole set of instructions are handed to the parents. The children are excited, as it will be the first time they will be away from home on their own. Although they are a bit nervous as the day for their departure nears, they are happy to have their friends with them so they will not be lonely. The mothers collect their immunization records. What a long word. Wonder what it means. Possibly, money station? I heard the children whine endlessly about getting shots and how much it hurts, and on and on. However, I did not go to any money station with them to get more bills. I will have to wait to learn about this word, I guess.

While the mothers are busy packing their boxes, the fathers help to label their clothes, suitcases, and backpacks. The children sneak in some snacks, including granola bars and chips. Mom gives Terry a very special gift: a diary to record the events of every day of her stay at camp. What a wonderful thought! Sid gets new hiking shoes and dark glasses. He tries them on immediately, and everyone says he now looks like the archeologist he wants to become! Again, one of those long words! Did I hear archieologist? Yet again, I wonder what that means. Perhaps, one who reads Archie comics? SS points out that Sid already reads them voraciously. Now, now, that is too many big words for me, and none of this is making sense yet.

Being the oldest and most responsible, Dad hands Terry pocket money, and we now find ourselves in her backpack along with a $5 and a $10 bill. I hope they will not be snooty! On the contrary, the $5 bill is looking rather crushed. She is so meek and unwilling to un-scrunch herself. To top it all, she is upside down—like she doesn't want us to see her. The $10 bill tells us that her name is one of the reasons she has become so shy and withdrawn. Her actual name is Jill Theodore March, but it has become shortened to "Jill Ted." Oh, dear! How could this be? She is teased for being "jilted" in love. I hope you know what that means—I sure do, for once. It means rejected or abandoned, especially by a lover. It is rather mean to call someone "jilted," don't you think? I realize immediately that we need to cheer her up.

Fortunately, Terry remembers she has to keep the money tucked away in her backpack carefully, so she smooths all of us out quite lovingly and rights Jill (notice how I only use her first name.) Honestly, I find Jill's smile quite bewitching. Hey, bewitching does not mean she is a witch. Oh, I know this word, too! Can you believe it? Two in a row today! Bewitching means captivating or delightful.

We are now on our way to Camp Destiny. We are received by the director and the young counselors at the camp. Parents are asked for the children's names and *immunization* records. I get it, I get it! *Immunization* has nothing to do with money. It is the shots the children complained about. This is to protect them from getting sick.

Counselor Don Keison takes charge of Sid and Matt, while Dee Livery takes the girls, Terry and Sara, with her. We bills laugh at the counselors' names. Imagine if the names were combined—they would become Donkei son and Deelivery. Ha ha! Somehow we don't get caught, even though laughing so hard. We are on a bumpy ride in Terry's backpack. Parents accompany the children to help unpack their stuff into little drawers and make their bunk beds. Matt's mom is teary-eyed as she leaves her baby Matt for the first time. He has his favorite blanket. Children rush to say their goodbyes, as they are excited to settle in. An orientation song and dance evening is planned for them.

As the sun goes down, the campers assemble around a campfire and sitting together in color-coded teams. They are wearing CAMP DESTINY T-shirts in two different colors. That explains the teams. Red for Terry and Sara, and Blue for Sid and Matt. Oh, it feels so cozy around an actual open-air fire.

Each team has come up with a goal to pursue in this one week. The girls have chosen to "not whine or complain" by enjoying all aspects of the camp with a positive attitude. The boys have decided to "show respect" for their counselors and elders by obeying all the rules. Well, we shall see who breaks their intentions first! Both teams are awarded 100 points today. Points will be subtracted as the intentions are broken. Winners will be announced on the last day, when there will be a talent show to be held in front of the parents. Sounds fair so far, right?

The rules call for lights out for bedtime at 8 p.m. sharp and a wake-up whistle at 6 a.m. sharp. To the kids, this seems like torture! The children face these rules bravely with a smile so as not to lose points. Counselors are lenient that night and pretend they don't hear the campers whispering in the dark and making new friends. In fact, the kids sit up and polish off their smuggled chocolates and snacks. A repartee— maybe like having a night party?

The next morning, after a delicious and heavy breakfast, the campers in hiking boots are herded through different trails in the mountains. If they don't follow their counselors, it is easy to get lost. I am a bit scared. It seems so eerie, as all the paths look the same surrounded by such tall trees. The children must learn the names of at least three rare trees and three rare flowers during this nature hike. Oh, dear, where is Sara looking? She is fascinated with one of the flowering tall trees. She can barely see the tree top. Looking upwards, she trips on a protruding stone and falls facedown with a scream. Although her knees are grazed, she is quite embarrassed to make a fuss. Terry helps her up and they both laugh it off. No minus points there, as she did not complain or whine.

Later that night, Sara draws Dee a picture of the rare tall tree. Terry calls her a "suck-up!" Jill remarks to MJ that the hungry children are eating their dinner voraciously. So voraciously must mean "a lot," as the children eat heartily and pretty fast.

Mountain biking is on the agenda for the next day. This time girls and boys are instructed to follow the same path behind their respective counselors. The teams tee off a few minutes apart, and the boys go first this time. Some of the paths are curved and close to the ledges. As it is, I am too scared of heights, so this is going to be one scary ride. Terry's team takes off just five minutes after Sid's, but when they reach the cliff top, there is a lot of commotion. The boys are off their bikes, crowding around someone. Terry jumps off her bike and screams as she finds Sid facedown on the ground, very close to the edge.

Apparently, a bump from a protruding root has sent Sid hurtling off his bike towards the edge. Counselor Don tells Sid not to move. Help is on the way. Counselor Dee quickly ties a rope to a tree and then around Don's waist. Don inches on his  stomach towards Sid, grabs him by the hand, and pulls him to safety. Whew, that was close! Sheepishly, Sid smiles as Terry gives him a big hug and tells him how fortunate he is. He could have been thrown over the edge! His skeleton might have been recovered by future archeologists, instead of him becoming an archeologist. Oh, so archeology is not about Archie comics. It means the study of remains and ancient history. I wonder if Team Blue will lose any points. Maybe not, as they are following instructions, and accidents are bound to happen.

The next morning, boating is on the schedule. Four boats accommodate the two teams. Children learn to row with oars in unison, and after some practice, all the boats land in the center. The boaters decide to have a friendly race. The lake is filled with cheering cries from the children as they try to go out to shore and meet back at the center. Being beginners, the boats do not turn around. Children are so smart! They just turn themselves around and row backwards. It is fun to see them struggle with much giggling and laughing. After much turning and reverse rowing, the boats assemble in the center again. No one is declared a winner, as too much time has elapsed. Suddenly, one of the girls screams, "Spider!" She jumps and stands up in her boat. Girls are such screamers! The boat almost capsizes. It takes an effort by the counselor to get her to sit down calmly and not rock the boat so much. Oh, dear, minus points await!

During the picnic lunch, the campers learn to barbecue on a grill. In the afternoon, they get to try out pedal boating. After strenuously rowing in the morning, this feels like a leisure activity. However, I see the boys in a huddle. They must be up to some mischief. It does seem a little suspicious, if you ask me. Gosh, I am so right. SS secretly indicates to me that the boys have hatched a plan to tease the girls. SS snickers at MJ's immediate repartee that the girls will win this round, as the boys will lose points. I now get it. Repartee is not about a repeat party; it is a quick reply. MJ is so smart.

Boys and girls are paired off into the pedal boats. As they pedal off, moving apart, a short boy whistles as a signal to the boys. When the girls pedal forwards, the boys pedal backwards. It is funny to see the pedal boats go round and round in the same place. Some of the boats actually go nowhere, not even around, even though the kids are pedaling furiously. Ha ha! On another whistle, each boy jumps up and screams

"Spider!" to scare the girls. Well, the girls are ready this time. They push off to shore before the boys can sit back down.

It is raining the next day, so indoor activities are planned. The campers have to make posters and come up with a talent show for their parents. The boys plan a karate demonstration while the girls practice a tap dance. Together, they decide to do a skit about avoiding homework. At least they agree on something! Actually, it is a relief for Jill and me to see a truce between SS and MJ, too. By evening, it stops raining, so the campers are taught to make s'mores, also known as *some mores*, around a campfire. They are so delicious: graham cracker sandwiches with melted chocolate and marshmallows. We bills have a way of finding sticky fingers—so yummy! Counselors engage the campers with spooky stories. Most of the children are happily falling asleep in different sitting postures. The counselors will have to help them to their bunks soon.

Parents start arriving to see their children with happy smiles. They hear about all the fun events and activities. The talent show is a huge success. In fact, some parents shout "Bravo!" Seeing my puzzled expression, Jill tells me this does not mean brave. It means they are praising the artists. The winners will soon be announced. I am so hyper that I can hardly wait. I see Dee and Don take the stage. They jointly announce that Team Red has 85 points, and after a long pause, they further announce that Team Blue is tied, with 85 points, too! Wow, how did that happen? So, all are declared winners. Prizes are little "Camp Destiny" badges to be sewn on their shirts for next year. They will no longer be novices or beginners, but veterans at Camp Destiny then.

Addresses, telephone numbers, and emails are hurriedly exchanged. It is so hard to part from each other, as the children have made so many new and dear friends this week. They plan to stay in touch and meet again same time next year at Camp Destiny. They could spend maybe two weeks together then. Sara is actually crying about having to part from her bunk buddy, Myra. It is so hard to bid goodbye. I sure understand that through all my adventures. Counselors hug their teams after a group picture is taken. They are always amazed by how tall the children have grown the following year.

Parents are very happy to have their young ones back, even though the cars are packed with piles of dirty laundry. The kids have been missed! Terry slides towards Mom and admits that every night, she secretly has been making entries in her diary. Before summer is over, she promises to share some, though not all, of her writings with Mom. Mom smiles knowingly and is very happy her gift is being used. She remarks that every child needs to keep a diary. Their innermost thoughts find a voice that way. Gosh, she is all-knowing and so correct. Maybe sometime I will disclose Terry's thoughts, writings, and confidences if you promise to keep it private and confidential.

Personally, I have had so much fun at camp with the children. Terry did not need any money while at camp, so we got to savor the food served and participate in all the fun activities. I hope I get to attend camp again next year. Until then, happy camping! Don't get too wild! Stay safe and have fun!

—————- $ —————-

Activities

1. Write letters to your camp friends and ask them what camps they plan to attend next year.

2. Make a list of all the things you liked and disliked at camp. Share it with your parents. It will help them to make decisions next year.

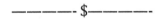

—————- $ —————-

- 24 -

UDB Celebrates the Fourth of July

What is special about July Fourth? Yes, today is our Independence Day and it is celebrated with parades, picnics, and fireworks! Oh, I am so excited, as My Lady has made plans to go downtown Washington, DC to the National Mall to see the fireworks. Whoopie! I can hardly wait.

I wonder how we are going to get there. It is too far to walk, so, the family car is loaded. Just as we back out from the driveway, My Gentleman realizes the driver's side tire is flat. Now what? My Lady suggests we take the bus to the Metro station. Here comes a bus. After dropping a whole bunch of noisy coins, we fall into seats up front. About halfway to the Metro Station, the bus stalls. Oh my! The bus driver tells us that the bus has broken down. He arranges for taxis to take us onward. Fortunately, we have a jovial taxi driver, who keeps us entertained with his non-musical whistling. It is a rather silly tune that he has us all rattling along with him singing and re-singing "Happy Birthday, America."

We are nearly there when the cops stop us. I cannot imagine that singing "Happy Birthday, America" is a crime. What did we do wrong, then? Apparently, there are road closures due to the local fireworks. Whew, that is a relief. We are asked to get out. The taxi driver refuses his fare, saying he is giving us a free ride, as it's Independence Day. Some people are just so generous!

We walk a short distance to the Metro station. I am afraid I will be used to buy Metro tickets. Then I will miss the fireworks. That would be so sad. Luckily, only larger bills are used, so I am saved! That was a close call. The tickets are swiped at the turn stiles. It must be fun being a turnstile, turning round and round the whole day! Riding down the escalator, we find our way to the middle of the platform. Almost immediately, the little lights on the platform edge start flickering and there comes a long train with eight compartments. We board the fifth one when the doors open and run to take our seats. Have you ridden on a Metro train? It is great fun to look out the window and see sights whizzing by. The whole family is smiling and happy, and we are finally on our way.

I speak too soon and jinx it. The train is going through a tunnel, so it becomes dark and sinister outside. However, with the lights inside, people continue reading, working on their computers, texting, or doing whatever they're doing. The train is slowing and with a big thud, it comes to a dead halt right in the tunnel. The doors are locked and we feel like prisoners. This is a bit scary. A voice comes on the speaker system, informing us that this is temporary and we need to be patient. I can barely understand the announcer with so much static in the background. Patience from us at a time like this is asking for too much as we are having a bad transportation day as it is. Fortunately, the air conditioner kicks in, and we feel less stifled. As no food is allowed on the trains, people are sharing and distributing their bottled water. The passengers are kind and friendly people.

Now I am getting really impatient. When will we get there? I hope we will not miss the fireworks after so many crisis situations. After what seems like an eternity, the train starts back up and we reach our station. Have you noticed that when you keep watching the clock, time feels like it is stretching? Looks like everyone is heading to the same place as the compartment empties out. I guess we just need to follow the crowd.

We find a great spot on the grass near the Washington Monument. People are sitting on blankets, portable chairs or directly on the grass. No one seems to mind shifting to make room for more viewers. We sit on our blankets, hardly able to contain our anticipation. I peek out every so often to see if the fireworks have begun.

All around, I see a sea of flags being waved by people. Everyone is wearing red, white, and blue. "How *patriotic,*" says My Gentleman. Sounds like some kind of rocket. Faces are painted with stripes on one side and stars on another. Again, this is about our national flag, nicknamed the "Stars and Stripes." A huge TV screen is broadcasting a concert taking place behind us in front of the Capitol building. Pointing to the screen, I hear My Gentleman tell My Lady to watch the famous Beach Boys perform patriotic songs. Aha! So *patriotic* must mean devotion to one's country. I hear the familiar "Yankee Doodle" song, and we bills hum along, with our edges waving. Children are wearing red, white, and blue neon necklaces and waving neon wands, too.

It is ice cream and popcorn time. Even these are in red, white, and blue flavors and cartons. The wallet is getting lighter, with $5 and $10 bills being used. I find myself expanding trying to straighten out my scrunched parts. I am happy to taste the ice cream, but I skip the popcorn.

The sun is down, and suddenly we hear an explosion in the skies. The people in front of us stand up, and our view of the Washington Monument is partially blocked. Everyone is in a good mood, so when My Lady politely asks them to sit down so we can see, they immediately oblige. I now realize that it does not matter who we are and from where we come—a little politeness and respect for each other goes a long way. Humans are inherently very nice and caring people.

Twenty minutes fly by so fast until the finale. This is the best part. There is so much noise and there are so many lights, shapes, and colors in the sky. It actually matches the different vibrant colors of all the viewers around us. With smoke high up in the air, it feels like the debris will fall on our heads, but it is actually quite far away. The colorful displays of mostly shades of red, white, and blue fireworks silhouette the Washington Monument. The fireworks form smiley faces, the letters U-S-A, a map of the USA, the world globe, flowers, fountains, and such images in vivid colors high up in the sky. What a memorable sight! I will keep it forever in my memory bank.

I hear applause all around. That must mean it is over. Must that be so? The Metro stations are extremely crowded, so they have officers staggering entries. Metro trains are operating almost every minute. The crowds clear pretty fast. We are now homeward bound. Free taxi rides are offered from the Metro station to homes. The children are so tired that they fall asleep. What a wonderful tiredness, though.

Even though we started out having one challenging adventure after another, I would not give up seeing the best fireworks at the National Mall. It was absolutely awesome! Have you ever had a day when so much goes wrong, yet so much goes right in the end? The best part is what we remember most, right? All's well that ends well. Until next Fourth.

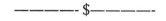

Questions/Activities

1. Where do you go to watch the July Fourth fireworks?

2. Have you ever visited Washington, DC to watch the fireworks? If you plan a visit, ask your parents if you can take a picture of yourself shaking hands with the President's life-size cutout.

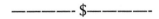

- 25 -

UDB Becomes a Foreigner

We welcome foreigners into our country, especially tourists. However, we never fully understand their feelings and inhibitions. One of their struggles is the way they need to adapt to strange customs and traditions and not be hurtful to their hosts.

My Lady (ML) and My Gentleman (MG) are invited to attend a Congress in Asia. This does sound like a great honor, doesn't it? Of course, we, the Three Billeteers ($1 bills) (Billie May, August Bill, and YT—not Yummy Tummy or Yuppy Toad or Yukky Troublemaker, but Yours Truly, Unique Dollar Billy) are excited. Friends native to the foreign country and some of their tourist friends give them a lot of tips, but I can see that ML and MG are determined to discover and form their own impressions. We now find ourselves crushed together with some foreign currency. We scrunch up to one side, and the scared foreign bills scrunch up the other side. This is not an amicable or friendly situation.

At the international airport, Bag 2 gets a push, and she flies down the automated carousel and lands on her four wheels. Before we know it, she is skating on all fours across the terminal, gathering speed with ML running behind her. Someone helps to carry her on to another carousel. Whoopee! She gets another free ride. ML is embarrassed and panting by this time and decides to wait at the opposite end of the carousel. As she points out her bag, six pairs of hands catch and pull her off the carousel. That must have been quite a ride. Children standing around the carousel laugh loudly and run to hold Bag 2 back so she doesn't trot off by herself again. Parents are happy that there is no early morning whining—just laughing and giggling. As for Bag 2, no more four-wheeling, dear. She is being dragged on two of her wheels to keep her in check.

When we are in a foreign place, it is easy to get lost, no matter how adventurous we are. ML and MG have to first learn the currency and the buying value of the money. They are mixed up trying to buy a cup of coffee. The bills are whispering. Are they making fun of their owners or pitying them? It is hard to tell when we are not seeing eye to eye. Suddenly, they start giggling as ML empties out her coins on the counter and lets the cashier take the correct amount. The bills are happy to get rid of their noisy, clinky counterparts, just as we always are. That breaks the ice.

One of my edges accidentally scratches a foreign bill. I jump to say sorry. Immediately, the foreigner smiles and shows me her full blue form. It looks different and unique, just like you and me! We become friends instantly, and I introduce her to my friends. She does the same, and there is much crackling and laughing as we realize there is so much to learn from each other. This is indeed going to be a fun trip.

We now have to deal with jet lag. Being younger than the $20 and $10 bills, we cope better. They seem sleepy all the time. Did you know that time varies in different countries? While flying east, we lose many hours—sometimes a whole day. Of course, we gain it back on the return journey. When it is day in the USA, it could be night out east. Even if the mind wants to stay awake, the body becomes lethargic and sleepy!

It's best to get some rest and adjust to the local time as soon as possible. We make a lot of noise to wake our elders. Otherwise, they will sleep through the day and keep us awake all night gossiping!

The next day, ML stops to ask directions in English. I did not realize that not everyone in the world speaks the same language. The person she stops tries to help her by saying something repeatedly, louder each time. It seems like she is barking at us. "Please don't shout, foreigner!" I want to say. I should take that back, because *we* are the foreigners in their country. We are not deaf—we just don't understand your language. All along, she is shouting, smiling, and waving her hands wildly. Maybe she is indicating that we are doing something wrong and she doesn't know English to let us know what it is. Meanwhile, another helpful lady who speaks broken English finally manages to give us directions.

We get hungry and ask for directions to a nearby Subway. I didn't realize the confusion until we land at the subway station and not the sub sandwich place, our favorite Subway shop. Buying train tickets is another challenge, as the instructions are in the foreign language. A kind gentleman helps, and we follow him through. We understand we must touch the ticket and not wait for the turnstile to open. So much can be said by the arms as he waves us to rush through. He holds out his fingers to indicate the number 4 to let us know when to get off. At the appropriate station, we stand back to watch other passengers exiting. The ticket must be put through a slot and cannot be reused. We will be experts at this shortly!

Let's then try to find something to eat, like a snack. Pictures do not always indicate all the ingredients, so if you have allergies like August does to peanuts, you are out of luck! Boy, he can sneeze his guts out sometimes. He gets more and more wrinkled each time! Poor fellow! Making food orders through a non-English speaking waiter is another dilemma. We find that most people in the country do not use cutlery. Some use sticks, while others use their hands to eat. We Billetteers jump, as we know we will get to taste everything as soon as the hands find their way to pay the bill. New food is exciting, and if one is adventurous enough to taste new spice mixtures and flavorings, life becomes more interesting. I bet ML and MG must have gone pretty hungry trying to balance food on the tips of their fingers or sticks. They eat some bread in a big hurry. The food smells delicious, and we taste the best parts greedily. Our foreign bills are quite at home and explain the dishes to us. My mouth is watering!

It is raining, and ML and MG have ventured out without an umbrella. Weather can be unpredictable, you know. They are using their hands and bodies along with trying to speak slowly. ML slips during her wave dance (not rain dance) and is saved from a fall by MG. Caught in time, I'd say. This may be true, but they are not dancing intentionally. They are gesticulating, trying to make themselves understood. Have you noticed that people think in their mother tongue and literally translate that into English while speaking? Nouns, verbs, tenses, and grammar get mixed up in the process. Hence, the use of arms and actions with words help.

The kind doorman teaches them a few words to facilitate shopping. Little do we know that the intonation and level of the sound changes meanings of words drastically from "thank you" to a scolding or to a horse! He tells us that bargaining is the only way to shop here. ML goes on a spree. Our foreign bills laugh when they see her trying to bargain. The shopkeepers have tripled the price for her, as they can tell she is a foreigner, so when she cuts them down a bit, they accept. She feels she has made a rare bargain, but only we know better. Our friends are so trusting and nice.

Only when I become a foreigner do I realize how isolated and odd one can feel. I will never treat my foreign friends in a way that makes them feel unsafe and unwanted. A friendly smile can go a long way. We are all foreigners somewhere or another, and it is these very differences that make us what and who we are. If we want to learn about other parts of the world and their cultures, we need to make travel fun and enjoyable. We need to be adaptable and accommodating. Seeing wondrous sights and views sometimes makes it hard to decide which we like better. Believe me, seeing pictures is not the same as seeing the real thing. Both man-made and natural sights can take our breath away.

Although the East tries hard to emulate the West, the traditional cotton, silk, indigenous, and polyester textiles are indeed magnificent. The traditional costumes and colors of the garb worn by the local people are practical to accommodate the climate of the place, and yet so vibrant and awesome. The history of the ancient civilizations, the geography of the lands, and the modernization of the cultures are all so intriguing. Oh, my, there is so much in this world to see, relish, and understand.

Going to foreign lands makes us more appreciative of "home." Traveling can be tiring, and we are relieved to finally arrive at home, sweet home. The children have missed their parents and want them to unpack immediately to see their gifts.

Are you planning a trip abroad soon? Be sure to take your passport and foreign currency. Bon voyage! Safe travels to your next destination!

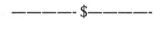

Questions/Activities

1. If you are going abroad with your parents, remind them to take the tickets, passports, and currency. Make a list of things you will need for travelling and at your destination.

2. Which country or city in the world would you like to visit, and why?

3. Are you learning any language in addition to English? If so, which one?

4. Find out what language is spoken in the country you want to visit and what currency is used there.

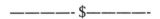

About the Author

———————❉———————

S ea Kay lives on the East Coast with her husband. Although scientific research has been her career, her passion is classical dance. With a blend of the science and arts, she has always been an advocate for education. After retiring from her day job, she was looking to reach out to children and decided to write creative short stories to stimulate their imaginations.

"My dream is to make children use their wildest imaginations. To envision a fun-filled future. To discipline their minds to break free from prejudice and other hateful actions and thoughts. They should aspire to be all they can be and whomever they want to be, with the appropriate sensitivities. Hence, I would like to formally introduce *UDB*."

This is her first writing endeavor aimed at stimulating the minds of children (ages 8–12 years). Soon, she hopes to read her stories aloud to her grandchildren, who are presently toddlers.

Sea Kay is very receptive to ideas and loves hearing from children, so please write to her at uniquedollarbilly@gmail.com

—————- $ —————-

CPSIA information can be obtained
at www.ICGtesting.com
Printed in the USA
FSHW011927250319
56666FS

9 781545 648049